P9-DME-321

This edition published by Parragon Books Ltd in 2015 and distributed by

Parragon Inc.
440 Park Avenue South, 13th Floor
New York, NY 10016
www.parragon.com

Copyright © Parragon Books Ltd 2015

Written by Steve Smallman   Illustrated by Simon Mendez

All rights reserved. No part of this publication may be reproduced, stored in a retrieval
system or transmitted, in any form or by any means, electronic, mechanical, photocopying,
recording or otherwise, without the prior permission of the copyright holder.

ISBN 978-1-4723-7582-7

Printed in China

Muddypaws'
Day at the Farm

PaRragon

Bath · New York · Cologne · Melbourne · Delhi
Hong Kong · Shenzhen · Singapore · Amsterdam

Ben and his puppy, Muddypaws, were best friends.
They loved playing together.

Ben liked playing with his toy tractor in the sandbox.

Muddypaws liked **digging** in the sandbox!

One morning, Muddypaws was playing
in the yard when Ben came rushing over.
"Muddypaws!" he shouted excitedly.

"Mom is taking me to visit a farm today ... and
you can come, too! We can feed all the animals,
and maybe we'll get to ride on a real tractor!"

Muddypaws was very excited when they got to the farm. There were so many new smells and lots of puddles, too! "I like it here!" thought Muddypaws. "It's **really** muddy!"

"Come on, Muddypaws!" cried Ben. "Let's feed the cows!"

Emile Gallé (French, 1846-1904)

Known equally for his exquisite glasswares (see pp.46-9), Emile Gallé's furniture is considered to be pure Art Nouveau. His inventive furniture designs heralded the rise of more floral decorative forms. He drew his inspiration from nature, particularly the flora and fauna of his native Lorraine. Gallé's work also led to a revival of marquetry.

Gallé's furniture

Gallé treated wood as a plastic medium, and did not try to follow the grain. His designs have a sculptural quality, as in the legs of the table in the main picture, which combine plant and animal forms, and show Gallé's fondness for dragonfly motifs. The tiers feature inlaid flowers and leaves.
* Designs include occasional furniture, as well as dining and bedroom suites. Some pieces are inlaid with verses (see p.47).

Gallé produced some novelty forms, such as the music stand, *above*, which adapted elements from other designs. This piece, from c.1900, is reminiscent of a Regency chiffonier, although it contains innovative variations that give it a strikingly original appearance. Characteristically, decoration appears on the sides and back as well as on the front. The quality of the fruitwood marquetry rivals that of the 18thC *ébénistes*. The motifs, of flowers and butterflies, are typical.

The form of the mahogany vitrine *above*, is simple, with emphasis on the inlaid and carved decoration, which itself is restrained. The shelves are undecorated. Larger pieces such as this (62in/159cm in height) generally command higher prices.

Identification

Gallé signed his work, usually in a corner, and often in elaborate inlay. After his death, the firm produced more traditional pieces, often with less inventive inlay. These are also signed ''GALLÉ''. However, they lack the originality of Gallé's own designs, although they command high prices in their own right. The craftsmen who executed his designs have not so far been identified.

Fakes and copies

Fakes and copies are not known to have appeared on the market. On occasion, some later pieces have been mistaken for copies, as a result of their restrained form.

Condition

Most of Gallé's furniture has survived in excellent condition: many pieces were commissioned, and owners have tended to covet each one. Even marquetry was laid so precisely as to have usually survived intact.

THE NANCY SCHOOL 2:
LOUIS MAJORELLE

A marquetry credenza by Louis Majorelle
c.1900; ht 89in/226cm; value code A

Identification checklist for Majorelle furniture
1. Is the piece architectural (featuring mainly inlaid decoration), or sculptural (with mainly carved decoration)?
2. Is decoration based on sinuous natural forms?
3. Are any carved motifs naturalistic?
4. Is the piece signed?
5. Is it hand-made?
6. Is it in an exotic or strongly grained wood, such as mahogany?
7. Is any marquetry of very high quality?
8. Is there a chicory leaf motif, inlaid or carved?
9. On chairs with arms, is the leg part of the armrest?
10. On sculptural pieces, has a lot of attention been paid to the supports?
11. Do pieces feature ormolu (gilt bronze) mounts, especially on the feet or supports?

Louis Majorelle (French, 1859-1926)

Majorelle took over his father's cabinet-making business in 1879. His early work was in a Rococo style but as a member of the Nancy School he was influenced by Gallé (see pp.12-3) and adopted Art Nouveau forms, creating an individual, elegant style. He favoured exotic and strongly grained woods, such as mahogany, and often used gilt bronze mounts. Like Gallé's, his decoration was based on sinuous forms and natural motifs.

On sculptural pieces, such as the carved mahogany side table *above*, decoration is often restricted to supports. These are reeded here, but fluted examples are also common, and legs usually terminate in slightly outswept feet. The wood grain is used to complement the design and to provide decoration.
* Mounts on sculptural pieces are often integral to the design.

Typical features and marks

The credenza in the main picture has the symmetrical form and inlaid decoration common to Majorelle's architectural pieces. Also typical are the short, solid feet and the supports (both embellished with metal mounts), the back panel, fitted with pleated silk, and the chicory leaf motif. There is an inlaid marquetry signature. Most of his work is marked, often on doors, and may be branded, stamped, inlaid or carved.

Collecting

Majorelle worked partly to commission, but also produced designs for a catalogue. Even so, his work is rare. Chairs with original fabric command a premium. As well as pieces in Majorelle's style, some unmarked items exist that may well have been designed by him. His work is well-documented and if in doubt collectors should refer to a documented example. His style was often imitated, which can be confusing to collectors, but fakes are so far unknown.

EUGÈNE VALLIN (French, 1856-1922)

Like Majorelle, Vallin was a cabinet-maker turned furniture designer, and a member of the Nancy School. He designed interiors, including ceilings, panelling and furniture. His pieces tend to be sculptural and imposing, with strong, curved, natural forms and decoration supplied by the natural wood grain. Sinuous stalk elements appear, often in supports.

Vallin's curvilinear forms are evident in the mahogany bureau and chair, *right*. The writing area is the only level surface. Stalk elements appear to evolve from the back plate. Mounts and handles are unobtrusive and the tapered supports have outswept club feet. Vallin's work is rarer than Gallé's or Majorelle's, but commands similar prices.

THE PARIS SCHOOL

A fruitwood salon cabinet by Eugène Gaillard c.1901-02; ht 72in/184cm; value code A/B

Identification checklist for the furniture of the Paris School
1. Is the form sculptural but relatively restrained?
2. Is the piece symmetrical?
3. Is it curvaceous, or does it contain a curved element?
4. Is it made of fruitwood?
5. Does any carving involve whiplash motifs in low relief?
6. Is the piece free of applied marquetry decoration?
7. If a chair, is any upholstery sympathetic to the form?

The Paris School
The two centres of French Art Nouveau design were Paris and Nancy. The designers of the so-called Paris School were associated with the Parisian publisher and dealer, Siegfried Bing (1838-1905), and his *Pavillon de l'Art Nouveau* at the Paris

Exhibition of 1900. Bing sponsored several designers, such as Georges de Feure (1868-1928), Eugène Gaillard (active 1895-1911), Edward Colonna (b.1862) and the architect Hector Guimard (1867-1942), who designed some striking entrances with organic motifs for the Paris Metro.

Forms

The Paris designers achieved a balance between elegant forms and strong organic elements, especially slender, sinuous stems or whiplash-type carving. Eugène Gaillard's large fruitwood salon cabinet, shown in the main picture, incorporates strongly curved, plant-like elements. The symmetrical form is typical of the Paris School.

* Gaillard produced bedroom and dining suites for the Paris Exhibition.
* Some of Gaillard's pieces include metal inlay.

Paris School designs tend to be traditional and restrained. However, many pieces incorporate both traditional and innovative elements, as does the chair, *above,* with its elongated back. Paris School chairs rarely include stretchers, but slender cabriole-type feet are fairly common. Here, carved decoration is limited to the edges, with a whiplash motif at the top of the seat rail.

* Edward Colonna, the designer of this chair, emigrated to the United States in 1882, but returned to Paris in the 1890s, where he created a drawing room for Bing's pavilion. He also designed jewelry for Bing and for Tiffany's as well as ceramic tablewares, produced at Limoges. He designed railroad car interiors in the United States and furniture for Canadian Pacific Railways in Montreal.

Hector Guimard's furniture is more sculptural than that of other Paris designers, and he often made clay maquettes which were translated into wood. As with the pearwood chair, *above,* Guimard's designs of 1900-10 were more gently curved and more sparsely decorated than his earlier work. He often used dark mahogany.

Georges de Feure's furniture tends to be either ornate or, like the cherrywood chair, *above,* remarkably restrained. Typical features include stylized floral and organic carved motifs, and simple white cotton upholstery, although he also often used embroidered silk or damask. He often highlighted his furniture with lacquerwork or gilt, and used pale woods in decorative combination with veneered figured panels.

17

HENRI VAN DE VELDE

An extraordinary oak, bronze and leather desk and chair,
designed by Henri Clemens van de Velde
c.1898; ht 50in/128cm; wdth 105in/267cm; value code A

Identification checklist for Henri van de Velde furniture
1. Does the piece incorporate both curved and straight lines?
2. Is it relatively restrained, and free of applied decoration?
3. Is the form balanced?
4. Does the design combine original forms with traditional influences?
5. Is the piece substantial in appearance?
6. Is it sculptural?
7. Are any metalwork fittings sympathetic to the piece, and perhaps of whiplash form?
8. Does any upholstery have beaded studwork?
9. Is the piece practical?
10. If a chair, are any splats slender?
11. Are any feet chamfered, and curved slightly outwards?

Henri Clemens van de Velde (Belgian, 1863-1957)
Henri Clemens van de Velde trained as a painter, architect and graphic designer in Antwerp and Paris, and was instrumental in the evolution of the Belgian Art Nouveau style. He designed all manner of items, including whole interiors, but was particularly influential in the fields of furniture, ceramics, jewelry and metalwork. His work was produced mainly to commission.

pieces of van de Velde furniture are chamfered, and may curve outwards slightly.

Availability
Van de Velde's furniture is fairly difficult to come by and, as his importance as a designer has now been fully recognized, is today keenly sought after. His ceramics, metalwork and jewelry tend to be more readily available.

Marks
Although porcelain designs by van de Velde are usually marked, his furniture rarely is. However, contemporary photographs of his work exist, which facilitates the search for the provenance of some pieces.

Innovation versus tradition
Van de Velde used innovative elements in his work, such as the curvilinear construction of the desk in the main picture. However, his work avoids being bizarre by the tempering of the innovative features with strong traditional elements.

Van de Velde's furniture designs
Van de Velde's furniture tends to be substantial, with restrained, sculptural forms. In the manner of the Paris School, pieces rely on form for interest, rather than the applied decoration and inlay commonly used by adherents of the Nancy School. Practicality is never sacrificed for the sake of design – the drawers of this unusual desk are all within easy reach. Rather, design works with function – the light fitting of this desk is incorporated into the piece. The electrical wire is trained through the metal gallery rail at the back of the desk. The railing is in a whiplash form, a common theme for his metalwork fittings.
* The unusual desk chair echoes the fluid architectural forms of the French architect, Hector Guimard, rather than the work of Art Nouveau cabinet makers such as Louis Marjorelle (see pp.14-5).
* The leather upholstery of the desk chair is characteristically decorated with beaded studwork.
* The chair feet are simple. However, the feet on some other

The armchair *above* has a traditional feel, despite the innovative interplay of uprights and horizontals. The way in which the arm rests overlap the upright back rails is typical of van de Velde's work, as are the slender splats and generally spartan design and decoration.
* The chair shows a Viennese influence in the union of form and function.
* Van de Velde also designed some chairs in cane; others were upholstered in leather or corduroy.

*A mahogany bronze-mounted coiffeuse by Serrurier-Bovy
c.1899; ht 74in/188cm; value code B*

Identification checklist for the furniture of Serrurier-Bovy
Early furniture (c.1900)
1. Is the design relatively ornate?
2. Is the piece mahogany?
3. Does it have a branded signature?
4. Are the fittings prominent, ornate and distinctive?
5. Is there any applied brass or bronze decoration?
6. Are the feet joined by arched stretchers?

"Silex" furniture (post-1902)
1. Are pieces in pale wood, such as pitch pine?
2. Is there any stencilled decoration?
3. Is the form relatively simple?
4. Do the joints incorporate raised metal studs?
5. Does the decoration employ circles and/or squares, combined with decorative lines, laid out in a symmetrical arrangement?
6. Does the piece incorporate painted tin plate?

Gustave Serrurier-Bovy
(Belgian, 1858-1910)

Born in Liège, Serrurier-Bovy became one of Belgium's leading Art Nouveau designers. His early work owes much to French and English design, particularly that of William Morris and the Arts and Crafts Movement, and pieces tend to be symmetrical, with restrained curves. He worked mainly in mahogany. The mahogany coiffeuse in the main picture, from c.1900, is typically architectural in form. Although solid, forms are often enlivened by the use of brass fittings, and curved elements.

Serrurier-Bovy's later work owes more to German or Viennese design. From 1902, he produced the "Silex" range of ready-to-assemble furniture in kit form.

* Serrurier-Bovy's clocks are also architectural, and often feature brass appliqués, with Arabic numerals inscribed onto Loetz glass (see pp.56-7).

"Silex" furniture

Serrurier-Bovy's inexpensive "Silex" range came about through his belief that everyone should have access to beautiful furniture. Pieces included tables, chairs and bedroom furniture. The night table, *below*, is typical in its use of simple geometric forms, pale wood, painted sheet metal, stencilled motifs and decorative studs.

Serrurier-Bovy produced many lamps, as well as hat and umbrella stands and ceiling lights in the style of that *above*. The use of horizontal bands – in this case, three toward the base and two below the shade – is typical. There is no surface decoration, but the minimalist design incorporates some florid features, such as the curving vertical side-pieces and the D-shaped spurs on the top rim of the shade. The screwheads on the lower horizontals are left exposed.

* Metalwork vases were made, usually combined with glass.

Marks and value

Serrurier-Bovy's work is usually signed, often with a branded signature. Silex furniture is stamped "SILEX".

* As when first made, Silex furniture is less expensive today than other Serrurier-Bovy pieces.

21

THE WIENER WERKSTÄTTE

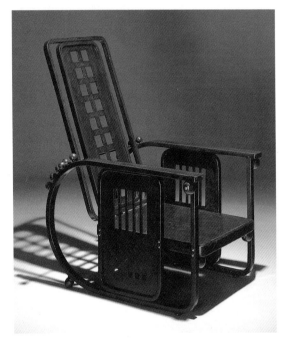

A beechwood chair designed by Josef Hoffmann for the Wiener Werkstätte c.1905; ht 42in/106.5cm; value code B

Identification checklist for furniture designed by Hoffmann for the Wiener Werkstätte (Vienna Workshops)
1. Is the piece of geometric or linear form?
2. Is use made of ball motifs, perhaps at intersections?
3. Do the decorative motifs include pierced squares or slender rectangular grilles?
4. Is the piece free of integral surface decoration?
5. When made from bentwood, is the piece devoid of angular corners (or are the corners gently rounded)?

Josef Hoffmann (Austrian, 1870-1956)
Originally trained as an architect, Hoffmann was influenced by Mackintosh (see pp.28-9) and the Glasgow School. His notable commissions include the interior of the Fledermaus cafe in Vienna. In 1897 he founded the Vienna Secession, an association of artists and architects disillusioned with the work of the Viennese Society of Visual Artists.

The Wiener Werkstätte (Vienna Workshops) (1903-32)
Inspired by the attempts of the Vienna Secessionists to bring more abstract and purer forms to design, Hoffmann founded the Wiener Werkstätte. Associated designers included Josef Maria Olbrich and Koloman Moser. As well as buildings and furniture, the group designed silver, glass (see pp.60-1), ceramics (see pp.82-3) and metalwork.

Hoffmann's designs

Hoffmann designed all kinds of furniture, including tables, chairs and light fittings. His work uses severe, geometric forms rather than the sinuous curves of other Art Nouveau designers. The *Sitzmachine* (sitting machine), in the main picture, typically combines simple oval and rectilinear forms. This example is adjustable – the knobs determine the angle of incline. Others have upholstered backs. This piece is made from beechwood, but Hoffmann often used more costly limed oak, mahogany and ebonized woods. The bases of some of his pieces are covered in beaten brass.

Some of Hoffmann's furniture is made in bentwood, that is, laminated or solid wood steamed and bent into the required curvilinear shape. Hoffmann's bentwood pieces typically have smooth or gently rounded corners. This simple bentwood table, *above*, is an example. It was made to Hoffmann's design by Jacob and Josef Kohn, one of the largest Viennese furniture manufacturers. Kohn, and another large Viennese firm, Thonet Brothers, executed the majority of Hoffmann's designs. Unlike many Wiener Werkstätte designers, Hoffmann took advantage of mass production techniques.

Josef Olbrich (Austrian, 1867-1908)

Olbrich's designs are not as severely geometric as those of Hoffmann and Moser, but are lighter, and feature formalized decorative motifs. Olbrich's walnut cabinet, entitled *Herbst* (Autumn), *above*, is made up of strong symmetrical elements. Decoration is restrained, consisting of panels inlaid in fruitwood and mother-of-pearl, and carved lines along the side.

The Wiener Werkstätte made several mantel clocks. The strongly geometric example *above*, by Josef Urban, is made of such diverse materials as walnut, silver plate, ivorene, enamel and agate.

Marks

Wiener Werkstätte furniture is seldom signed. Attribution is usually made using contemporary photographic or original design material.

CARLO BUGATTI

*A vellum-covered bench seat by Carlo Bugatti
c.1900; ht 58in/148cm; value code A*

Identification checklist for the furniture of Carlo Bugatti
1. Does the piece exhibit a Moorish influence?
2. Does decoration incorporate embossed metal appliqués, or ivory or pewter inlay?
3. Is the form highly inventive, and perhaps sectional?
4. Is the piece signed?
5. Does the design make use of a variety of woods and/or decorative materials?
6. Does it make play of geometric motifs, particularly medallions?
7. Does any upholstery incorporate vellum, perhaps painted with Arab figures or scenes?

Carlo Bugatti (Italian, 1855-1940)
Bugatti came to public attention when he designed the Moorish interior for the Italian section at the Turin International Exhibition of 1902. His individual style was based on extravagant ornamentation, geometric shapes and Moorish themes. His designs, as much works of art as pieces of furniture, earned him a reputation as Italy's leading furniture designer.

Decoration

Although influenced by North African styles, Bugatti's decorative approach was highly original, with strong play on geometric motifs, particularly circles or roundels; the side chairs of the bench seat in the main picture have backs in the form of circular shields. Bugatti used a large variety of materials in decoration and was particularly fond of incorporating brass, pewter or ivory inlay. The standard of inlay is invariably high; indeed, it was often more inventive and of higher quality than the North African models that inspired him. Bugatti also applied to his furniture strips of beaten or pierced metal, or embossed metal appliqués and tassels. His use of vellum (fine calf or lambskin parchment) was particularly unusual and characteristic; the bench seat in the main picture is covered in vellum decorated with Japanese motifs. Seat backs are often decorated in a similar fashion.

Bugatti's furniture

Bugatti produced a wide range of furniture, often for a specially commissioned interior. Interest in his work grew with increased European colonial expansion into North Africa and the resultant exposure to the Arab culture. Many of his interiors have a decadent, harem-like appearance, reinforced by the addition of exotic Middle Eastern carpets.

Forms

The bench seat in the main picture combines strong circular and rectilinear elements, the various sections defined by elaborate, turned uprights. The strong verticals, many of which protrude from the piece, are typical. Evidently comfort was not always his primary aim.
* The elements of large sectional furniture were often produced as separate pieces.

Cabinets, such as this ebonized and rosewood writing desk, *above*, are also architectural in form and make strong use of pillars and spindles. Some pieces combine function and form – for example, tables may incorporate cabinets, and seats may be designed with integral lamps.
* Colours tend to be subdued; brown and black dominate.
* Turned legs often have blocks at terminals or junctions.

A green-stained oak writing bureau designed by C. A. Voysey 1896; ht 59in/149.5cm; wdth 43in/110.5cm; value code B/C

Identification checklist for Voysey furniture

1. Is the form highly individual, with an architectural feel and a vertical emphasis?
2. Is the piece hand-made?
3. Does it employ woods native to England, such as oak or beech, possibly stained?
4. Is any decoration pierced, possibly with a heart motif?
5. Is the natural wood grain used to decorative effect?
6. Are any decorative motifs of the flowing, organic style associated with Continental Art Nouveau?
7. Is use made of metal appliqués or painting?
8. Is there any inlay, in wood or metal?

Charles Annesley Voysey (English, 1847-1941)
Originally trained as an architect, Voysey designed buildings and whole interiors, mostly to commission. He adopted a style strongly influenced by the English Arts and Crafts movement. His furniture was hand-made in native woods such as oak and beech, and he sometimes used stained wood, as in the writing desk in the main picture. His distinctive designs tend to have a strong vertical emphasis, usually created by the use of long, tapering, upright elements, such as the octagonal columns supporting the desk. These sometimes terminate in rectangular finials, like those on the oak games table *right*. Chair

backs, which can be very innovative in design, also tend to incorporate tapering uprights, perhaps at right angles to the arm rests.
* The overhanging top of the writing desk is characteristic of Voysey.

Decoration
Voysey's designs are always well balanced and solid looking, partly due to the harmonious decoration, which tends to be symmetrical, giving the item a balanced appearance. Voysey's pieces rely mainly on the wood grain and their unusual design for decorative effect. Any additional decoration is usually pierced or inlaid, but may be painted or in the form of metal appliqués. Motifs are generally entwined in a flowing organic style with obvious roots in Continental Art Nouveau. The central metal hinge of the writing desk in the main picture is pierced with the figures of two birds and a snake in a typical Art Nouveau style.

The card suit motifs on the games table, *above*, are inlaid with copper, an unusual material for Voysey, who tended to prefer brass for inlay and attachments such as handles. The heart motif appears here as one of the card suits, but Voysey often used the heart in his work, as did other designers of the period. Typically, the stretchers meet the uprights at the corners and are slotted in rather than tenon-jointed.

Identification
Voysey never signed his work, but many of his designs are registered at London's Patent Office. Despite imitators, his unique style is unmistakable.

MACKAY HUGH BAILLIE-SCOTT (English, 1865-1945)
Baillie-Scott was primarily an architect and his furniture generally tends to be architectural in execution.

Baillie-Scott designed robust, utilitarian furniture hand-made in mahogany and oak. He used the natural grain of wood to decorative effect. His best pieces employ inlays, usually symmetrical and sometimes bold and dramatic. The mahogany wardrobe *above*, made by the cabinet-making firm, Wylie and Lochhead, has chequered inlay in ebony and blond woods. Typically, the apron is curved and the cornice overhanging. Also characteristic are the panels outlined with ornate stringing – on this example the stringing echoes the chequered motif. Baillie-Scott frequently used metal inlay; pewter roundels, made to designs similar to that illustrated *below*, were especially characteristic of his work.

Identification
Baillie-Scott designed all manner of furniture, none of which is signed, and much is erroneously attributed to him. Contemporary photographs or magazine articles may help establish provenance.

C. R. MACKINTOSH

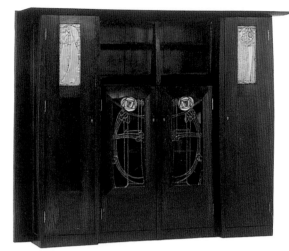

*An oak cabinet designed by Charles Rennie Mackintosh
1898; ht 63in/159cm; value code A*

**Identification checklist for the furniture designs of
Charles Rennie Mackintosh**
1. Does the piece have a vertical element or emphasis?
2. Is it symmetrical?
3. Is it made of oak, either stained to a dark colour or
white-painted?
4. Does decoration make use of a symbolic, shrouded
female figure?
5. If a cabinet, does it incorporate a decorative panel,
possibly using a stylized rose?
6. If a ladder-back chair, does the "ladder" extend
beneath the seat?
7. Does any piercing form a chequered design?
8. Are any brass fittings, such as handles or escutcheons,
subtle?

**Charles Rennie Mackintosh
(Scottish, 1868-1928)**
The architect-designer Charles
Rennie Mackintosh was one of
the most influential figures in the
development of Art Nouveau and
the Modern Movement. He was
admired on the Continent,
especially by the Viennese
Secessionists (see pp.22-3). He
worked closely with the architect
Herbert MacNair and the
Macdonald sisters, Margaret,
who later married MacNair, and
Mackintosh's future wife,
Frances, who designed

metalwork and embroidery.
Together they were known as
the Glasgow Four.

Furniture
Mackintosh designed mainly to
commission. His furniture has
clean lines and minimal
decoration. He often worked
with dark stained oak, as in the
large cabinet in the main picture,
but produced a number of
designs in white painted wood.
He also designed light fittings,
pianos, cutlery (flatware) and
wrought-ironwork.

Decoration

Decorative details may include painted or beaten brass panels and leaded and glazed windows. The oak cabinet in the main picture has a combination of these. The brass panels bear enigmatic female figures, a motif which earned the Glasgow Four the nickname of the "Spook School". One panel is signed "MARGARET MACDONALD". Macdonald married Mackintosh in 1900. The leaded glass panel is decorated with a stylized rose – sometimes known as a "Glasgow rose" – a motif used by Mackintosh and other Glaswegian designers. However, it was not exclusive to them – for example, it appears on mass-produced items such as Doulton stoneware (see pp.102-3).

the motif of a formalized bird in flight, is typical. Comfort was not a prime consideration. The chair is fitted with a rush seat. Upholstery tends to be very simple. The double spindle stretchers are typical, as are the side supports, which extend below the seat and above the back rest.
* This piece was designed for the dining room of Miss Cranston's Tea Rooms in Glasgow.

The contoured seat of this low-backed oak armchair, *above*, is typical of Mackintosh's wooden seats. Like the tall chair, it was designed for Miss Cranston's Tea Rooms, this example for the billiard and smoking room.

Beware

Mackintosh did not sign his work, although most of his designs are well-documented. A large amount of furniture is optimistically described by dealers and auctioneers as being "in the Mackintosh style", and his name is often used as an umbrella term for a variety of general Arts and Crafts-style furniture.
* In recent years his work has been reproduced by the Milanese firm of Cassina S.C.A.

Later work

Mackintosh's later commissions (those produced from c.1912 onwards) often incorporate elements of stringing or plastic materials and tend to be less exciting and less collectable than his earlier work. In 1920, he moved to France to pursue an interest in painting.

The high-backed oak dining chair, *above*, has a strongly perpendicular emphasis and a sculptural quality – common elements of Mackintosh's furniture. He was particularly fond of the tall, ladder-back form for chairs. He often applied decorative motifs to the back; this oval back rail, pierced with

THE COTSWOLD SCHOOL

*A walnut and ebony cabinet by Ernest Gimson
1908; ht approx. 4ft/1.23m; value code C*

Identification checklist for the furniture of Ernest Gimson
1. Is the form relatively simple?
2. Does the piece feature subtle inlaid decoration?
3. Is there an element of geometry in form or decoration?
4. Has use been made of veneers or contrasting woods?
5. Is the piece hand-made?
6. Is it a cabinet or an item of dining furniture?
7. Are elements in the construction reminiscent of medieval craftsmanship (see facing page)?
8. Has ebony been used?

The Cotswold School (1893-mid-1930s)
This loose association of English furniture makers, located first at Pinbury and then at Sapperton in the Cotswolds, Gloucestershire, was led by the architect and designer Ernest Gimson and the brothers Sydney and Ernest Barnsley. The School attempted to unite traditional rural crafts-manship with the handcrafting principles advocated by the Arts and Crafts Movement. Designs were relatively sombre, with decoration sometimes restricted simply to chequered stringing. However, each member of the group had his own distinctive style. Craftsmen associated with the Cotswold School include the Dutch cabinet-maker Peter Waals (1870-1937), who became foreman in 1901.

Gimson's furniture

Gimson's designs feature simple geometric forms, and have a strongly symmetrical emphasis. His work is typified by the use of figured and often contrasting woods. Gimson used both local and exotic woods, and had a particular fondness for ebony, which is featured in the large cabinet in the main picture. On many pieces, he achieved the decorative effect purely through geometric arrangement of the grain on areas of veneer. Heavy cabinets, such as the example in the main picture, tend to be supported on equally heavy, short feet. Although cabinets predominate, Gimson also made a small amount of dining room furniture, usually of relatively simple form.

* Ernest Gimson also produced a number of designs for execution in wrought iron, plaster and embroidery.
* Most of Gimson's work was designed to exclusive commission.
* None of his work is signed.

Rather than relying on just contrasting woods, or inlays of holly, ebony and cherrywood, some of Gimson's more expensive pieces also include inlaid ivory, bone or mother-of-pearl. The latter is featured on the cabinet *above* in the form of inset panels and a central escutcheon.

The Cotswold craftsmen spurned the use of screws in favour of the more traditional dovetail joints, clearly visible in the detail *above*, from the cabinet, *left*.

Sydney Barnsley (1865-1926) and Ernest Barnsley (1863-1926)

These brothers produced simple, well-proportioned, functional furniture, including dining and bedroom furniture and a range of occasional pieces. Using traditional methods, they avoided the use of screws, and preferred chamfered legs to sharp edges. Pieces are not signed and their work is hard to tell apart.

Like Gimson, the Barnsley brothers used the colour and the grain of the wood for decorative effect. However, the mahogany sideboard, *left*, designed by Sydney Barnsley, makes use of painted decoration by the ceramic decorators Alfred and Louise Powell. In addition to mahogany, the Barnsleys also used local woods, mainly walnut and oak. They are not known to have used ebony.
* The Barnsley works closed c.1918.

E. A. TAYLOR

An oak and leaded glass writing cabinet designed by E. A. Taylor
c.1903; ht 48in/121.5cm; value code B/C

Identification checklist for the furniture of E. A. Taylor
1. Is the piece architectural in form?
2. Is it made of oak, either stained, ebonized or painted white?
3. Is it solid and substantial?
4. Do pediments overhang?
5. Does the piece have leaded glass panels, perhaps inset with stained glass and with floral decoration?
6. Do handles form an important decorative element?
7. If a screen, is there wood panelling or a waved top rail?

Ernest Archibald Taylor (Scottish, 1874-1951)
Not as much is known of Taylor as of his fellow Glaswegian and friend, C. R. Mackintosh (see pp.28-9). However, as a painter and furniture designer he was influential in bringing the designs of the Glasgow School to a wider public. Few pieces were directly commissioned; instead, Taylor's furniture was made commercially, mostly by the firm of Wylie and Lockhead. In 1908, Taylor moved to Manchester to work for George Wragge Ltd.

Taylor's furniture

Taylor's designs are often confused with those of Mackintosh, but his work is more similar to that of the British Arts and Crafts designers. It is always substantial, with strong vertical elements and spare but distinctive decoration, and is usually made of stained, ebonized or white-painted oak. His work typically includes the overhanging pediments evident on the writing cabinet in the main picture. The leaded glass panels set into the upper cabinet of this piece are characteristic, as is the use of stained glass. These panels would have been designed by Taylor himself. The stylized rose design on this cabinet was a common motif. Mackintosh also used the rose motif.

* The tiny, pierced, formalized flowerheads on the bottom apron of this writing cabinet indicate Taylor's work, but are not exclusive to him.

Attribution

Taylor's furniture is rarely found at auction today. His pieces are not marked, so the collector must try to establish the provenance. Useful contemporary documentation includes the London-based design publication, *The Studio*. There are also numerous other British and Continental art journals and sources of information.

The white lacquer on the bureau *above* is original, a vital consideration in the valuation of Taylor's painted furniture. This example bears a strong stylistic resemblance to the writing cabinet in the main picture. The handles are typical, being of ring form, and provide the piece with a strong decorative element.

Screens

Taylor designed several screens, typically with an arched or waved top rail to the central leaf. These pieces tend to have wood panelling, rather than the fabric or stamped leather more commonly used at that time.

GEORGE WALTON
(Scottish, 1867-1933)

Walton studied architecture and design at evening classes at the Glasgow School of Art. He started his own interior design firm, George Walton & Co., Ecclesiastical & House Decorators, in 1888. Among his commissions were chairs in ebonized wood for the photographic firm, Kodak, and he began to work for Liberty in 1897. His designs, being strongly linear and with vertical emphasis, were influenced by the Glasgow School, of which he was a member.

The twin tapered backs provide a vertical element in Walton's oak settle, *left*. The heart-shaped motif on the backs is a hangover from the Arts and Crafts period.

* Walton produced a large amount of metalwork in iron and copper, and a range of Clutha glasswares for James Couper (see p.62-3).

A mahogany and stained glass cabinet, designed by G. Ellwood for J. S. Henry c.1900; ht 77½in/197cm, wdth 55in/140cm; value code C/D

Identification checklist for the furniture of J. S. Henry
1. Is the design architectural?
2. Is the piece relatively lightweight?
3. Does it combine Art Nouveau elements with traditional forms?
4. Is it inlaid?
5. Is it veneered in mahogany?
6. Is any decoration of stylized flowers?
7. Does the piece incorporate leaded and coloured glass window panels?

J. S. Henry (British, c.1880-c.1900)
The firm began cabinet-making in east London c.1880, mass-producing high-quality, mainstream furniture. It is best known for its "Quaint" furniture, a trade version of Art Nouveau that

combined elements of the Glasgow School (see pp.28-9), European Art Nouveau and Arts and Crafts. Pieces are architectural, lightweight and ornamental, and the range includes some fine mahogany-veneered items. Stylistically, the firm balanced the old and the new; the cabinet in the main picture marries classical elements – seen in the arches – with Art Nouveau features – such as the leaded glass window panels and the stylized iris decoration and inlay. Its designer, George Ellwood used more openwork than his colleagues. Along with E. G. Punnet, he is the most sought-after of Henry's furniture designers.

Value
Henry pieces are still relatively inexpensive, although many are of fine quality, like the cabinet in the main picture, whose value is enhanced by having appeared in a retrospective exhibition.

between 1900 and 1910.

Other features of English Art Nouveau furniture include stained pink wood, coloured glazed doors, mother-of-pearl inlay and metal inlays, including copper, brass and pewter.

Bath Cabinet Makers Co. Ltd. (English, dates unknown)
In the 1970s, a misinterpretation of the unusual forms, innovative Art Nouveau decoration and high standard of craftsmanship evident in much Bath furniture led to its being wrongly attributed to Liberty and others. This mistake has now been acknowledged.

The mahogany and marquetry cabinet *above* is by an unknown designer. However, as an experimental exercise in Art Nouveau, it could fetch as much as five times the price of the cabinet *left*. Again, it is a hybrid of various forms; the structure is similar to the work of Voysey (see pp.26-7), the decoration echoes van de Velde (see pp.18-9), the motifs on the panelled doors have a French influence, and the spindles owe something to Josef Hoffmann. It is typical of the experimental furniture produced in Britain

The firm worked mainly in light mahogany, and oak. Designs can be unusual: the vitrine *above* is octagonal and designed as an all-round piece, with no front. All sides are glazed. Other typical features include the stained and inlaid door panels with stylized floral designs, and the inlaid overhanging top. Bath used similar stylized floral decoration to J. S. Henry's, and rose motifs often echo the Glasgow Rose (see p.29).
* Most Bath furniture was sold through commercial outlets such as Heal's in London, and pieces often have a tag bearing design details. Unmarked work is hard to attribute, as little is known of the firm's designers.

An oak spindle-back side chair by Frank Lloyd Wright
c.1908; ht 46in/117cm; value code A

Identification checklist for the furniture designed by Frank Lloyd Wright

1. Is the form imaginative, with an architectural influence?
2. Does the design make use of rectilinear lines and intersecting planes?
3. Is any decoration integral to the form rather than applied to the surface?
4. Is wood furniture made of oak with either a reddish or brown patina?
5. If a stained-glass window, is the design geometric or abstract, and of vertical emphasis with scant use of colour?

Note
Wright's early work was hand-made, but later pieces were made commercially with metal screws and machined joints.

Frank Lloyd Wright (American, 1869-1959)

Wright was a prolific commercial and residential architect. He believed in thematic consistency in interior design and so created the furniture and furnishings for most of his architectural projects himself. Before 1914, he worked mainly in the distinctive "Prairie" style, a mid-Western interpretation of the Arts and Crafts movement, of which he was a major exponent. Working in stained, fumed oak with a dark, reddish patina, he created forms of revolutionary simplicity, based on architectural, rectilinear lines and intersecting planes, which relied on their imaginative construction for decorative effect. The undecorated spindles and slab crest rail of the chair in the main picture are typical. Wright's domestic designs tend to be prefered to his commercial work: not only are these pieces rarer and of more complex design, but they are usually better made. The progressive pieces are most popular, particularly spindle- and high-back seat furniture .

Metal and glasswork

From c.1905, Wright produced some painted sheet metal furniture, as well as metal vases and lighting fixtures in bronze and stained or leaded glass. He also designed stained-glass windows.

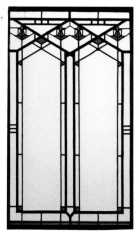

Stained-glass panels, such as this one, *above*, tend to be small-scale and designed with rectilinear panels of vertical emphasis. These sometimes include diagonals, as in the top section of this window, an arrangement inspired by the art of the American Indians. The use of colour tends to be minimal, and ornament abstract. The same treatment is found on some of Wright's light fixtures.

Fakes and reproductions

None of Wright's work is signed, but provenance is usually well documented. While no deliberate fakes exist, a good deal of contemporary American furniture is misrepresented as Wright's work, particularly stained glass and furnishings in the Prairie style, but these are identifiable by their inferior design. In recent years, some of Wright's early designs have been reproduced; these can be distinguished by their obvious newness.

Wright's late work

Wright's late work is inexpensive compared to his early pieces, but is bound to increase in value as the already limited supply of his early work becomes exhausted.

Most examples of Wright's work available today were designed for commercial interiors, such as offices and schools. This side chair was made for the Hillside Home School at Spring Green, Wisconsin. The simple structure and leather seat are typical.

THE GREENE BROTHERS

*A mahogany and ebony armchair designed by the Greene brothers
c.1907; ht 42in/107cm, wdth 24¾in/63cm; value code A*

**Identification checklist for the furniture of Charles and
Henry Greene**
1. Does the design show an Oriental influence?
2. Are joints complex and visible, involving squared,
wooden pegs of darker colour than the cabinet wood
(ebony and mahogany being the most common
combination)?
3. Is the form simple yet imaginative?
4. Is the standard of craftsmanship high?

**Charles Sumner Greene
(American, 1868-1957) and
Henry Mather Greene
(American, 1870-1954)**

The Greene brothers opened a
studio in Pasadena, California, in
1893 to design buildings,
furniture and furnishings. Their

style shows the influence of Arts and Crafts, of Japanese and Chinese construction standards and of the aesthetic theories of Frank Lloyd Wright (see pp.36-7), whom they admired. They worked exclusively to commission: the armchair in the main picture was designed for the Robert Blacker house in Pasadena. The Gamble House in Pasadena, completed by them in c.1909, is now a museum. The partnership was dissolved in 1916.

Materials and methods
The brothers worked mainly in Honduras mahogany. Joints are complex and visible, involving square pegs of a darker wood than that of the main piece; the chair, *left*, uses ebony and mahogany, a favourite combination. Decoration often involves square ebony pegging or inlay of metal or coloured wood.

Value
Being exclusive, their work is rare and collectable. Pieces are not signed, but are usually well-documented. Some designs have recently been commercially reproduced but these can be easily identified by their newness and inferior craftsmanship.

The brothers designed some lighting fixtures with leaded glass panels. Some are in the style of Tiffany (see pp.66-9).

The highly unusual frame of the iridescent beige and amber glass lantern *above*, is of mahogany embellished with ebony pegging, the distinctive Greene combination.

CHARLES ROHLFS (American, 1853-1936)
Charles Rohlfs opened his practice in Buffalo, New York, c.1890. His style is unmistakably Arts and Crafts-influenced, with extensive use of exposed joinery. As evident in the drop-front desk *left*, Rohlfs worked almost exclusively in dark oak, sometimes stained black, and made a feature of hand-wrought iron or copper hardware. As well as desks he produced storage chests, library furniture and sideboards. Most pieces bear an incised monogram, ''CR'', and some are dated, which collectors tend to prefer.

GUSTAV STICKLEY

An oak and leather library table designed by Gustav Stickley c.1902; ht 30in/76cm; lgth 65½in/167cm; value code C

Identification checklist for Gustav Stickley's furniture
1. Is the form extremely simple and rectilinear?
2. Is the wood riven and joined with mortice and tenon or other traditional techniques of carpentry?
3. Is the piece made exclusively of oak?
4. Is it solid and heavy?
5. Is any hardware hand-made, perhaps with a hand-hammered surface?
6. If the piece is upholstered, is the upholstery leather?

Stickley furniture
The Stickley name is associated with plain furniture in solid oak, often described as "Mission style", because of its similarity to pieces found in 19thC American mission churches. Furniture bearing the Stickley name can be attributed to one of three factories, the best known and most collectable of which is the firm of Gustav Stickley.

Gustav Stickley (American, 1898-present)
Gustav Stickley (1847-1942), opened a factory in New York State, to make original furniture

with an Arts and Crafts feel. The table in the main picture is typically simple and solid, its rectilinear construction designed to prevent warping or shrinkage. The firm used mainly American white oak, stained rich or light brown, or grey, using a fuming process developed at the factory. Traditional construction methods were used, as well as hand-made hardware, often with a hammered surface. The leathered top of the table *above* is held with brass tacks made in a 17thC manner.
* Upholstery is mainly leather, typically brown, red or green.

The music cabinet *below* is one of the rare designs by English-born architect and furniture designer, Harvey Ellis (1852-1904), who worked with Stickley from 1902. The inlaid panel is typical of Ellis's work; he often used Jugendstil-style motifs inlaid in contrasting materials, such as ivory or darker woods, as well as pewter and copper. Other motifs commonly include stylized flowers and Viking ships. Most inlaid Stickley pieces can be attributed to Ellis.

"Craftsman" furniture

This range, made from c.1900, included textiles, metalwork and some woven furniture in willow and oak. The most collectable, progressive designs evoke the work of Hoffmann or Mackintosh, notably the high-backed, spindled seat furniture.

Marks and reproductions

Most of Stickley's work is stamped in red with a joiner's compass device enclosing the Dutch motto "Als ik kan". The company still makes quality oak and cherry furniture in the Colonial style which presently is of no collectable value. They have recently reproduced a few of Stickley's early designs, but these are obviously modern.

Ellis's designs are so popular that some Stickley pieces have been fitted with modern inlay intended to deceive; poor quality of work usually identifies these.

The Stickley Brothers (1891-1910) and L. and J. G. Stickley (c.1900-present)

George and Albert Stickley, two of Gustav's younger brothers, had a workshop in Michigan, making oak furniture, similar to the Craftsman line, and conventional rustic "Quaint furniture". Neither type equalled Gustav's work in quality, nor are they of value today. Of more interest is the work of two other brothers, Leopold and J. George Stickley, who based their designs on later Craftsman models. They made simple, solid home and office furniture, such as bookcases and tables. The more progressive items are the most popular today. Many pieces bear a branded signature or brass plate.

GLASS

A crocus vase designed by Emile Gallé, c.1900

Of all the media available to Art Nouveau craftsmen, glass, by nature of its plasticity, offered the most opportunities for innovative design. Glassmakers abandoned the elaborate cutting advocated by previous generations and explored the medium, concentrating on sculptural and surface possibilities. The skills of chemists and master glass blowers, combined with the fertile imagination of designers, resulted in completely new and exciting forms.

In France, the town of Nancy was established as the cradle of French art glass production by the likes of master glassmaker Emile Gallé (see pp.46-9), and his admiring contemporaries, Auguste and Antonin Daum (see pp.50-1). Both Gallé and Daum Frères developed industrial mass-production techniques which helped make cameo glass more readily available to the masses. Of these industrial wares, the fire-polished or martelé-cut pieces are the most sought after today. However, it is the more exclusive studio glass (the one-off pieces made by designers and glassmakers working in collaboration) which command the highest prices. Studio glass tends to be far more spontaneous than the more rigid, uniform mass-produced wares.

Gallé's cameo designs were synonymous with Art Nouveau, although he also perfected the technique of *marquetrie de verre*, and experimented with new possibilities for glass surfaces, such as iridescence (see pp.46-9). The forms of Gallé and Daum glasswares were for the most part impressionistic, while decoration relied heavily on local flora, insects and other wildlife.

Outside France, in Austria and the United States, emphasis was laid on the use of controlled iridescent surfaces. American glass makers such as Victor Durand and the firms of Quezal (see pp.72-3) and Steuben (see pp.70-1) all catered for the craze for iridescent glass, which attempted to emulate the lustrous plumage of peacocks and hummingbirds. Indeed, the peacock feather motif was a source of inspiration for America's greatest glass artist, Louis Comfort Tiffany (see pp.66-9). Tiffany glass is highly collectable. However, except in the instance of Tiffany lampshades, the market for American glass has not kept pace with that for French wares. Small Tiffany pieces, such as salt cellars, are easily affordable. The Austrian glassworks of Loetz (see pp.56-7) produced glasswares similar to Tiffany's. For many years these were incorrectly regarded as inferior Tiffany lookalikes, but recent research has shown that Tiffany himself had long admired the work of Loetz.

In Britain, the challenge of Art Nouveau glass design was met by few glassmakers. Perhaps the most interesting wares are those produced by the Stourbridge glassmakers Stevens & Williams, and the small amount of cameo glass produced by Thomas Webb & Sons (see pp.64-5).

Meyr's Neffe, the Bohemian glassworks, produced a series of drinking glasses and useful objects such as table lamps, inspired by the geometric designs of the Austrian architect Otto Prutscher. In Sweden, the Orrefors glass factory made popular Graal glass perfected by Edward Hald and Simon Gate, while in Russia, the Imperial Glass Factory in St Petersburg produced cameo glass.

The death of Gallé in 1904 signalled the end of innovative Art Nouveau glass design. Production continued at Daum, but these later wares were clearly inspired by Gallé.

A substantial amount of faked Art Nouveau glassware has been discovered in recent years. Tiffany lamps have been faked in large numbers, and spurious Tiffany marks are often found on iridescent wares not produced by them. A range of cameo wares marked "Gallé" have surfaced in both France and Japan (where most fakes are thought to originate), but these are always stiff and lifeless, and lack vitality. Anyone used to handling genuine Gallé will automatically be suspicious. Some fake Loetz glass has also been discovered.

BURGUN, SCHVERER & CO.

*A Burgun, Schverer & Co. martelé glass vase
1895; ht 9½in/23.5cm; value code B*

**Identification checklist for the cameo glasswares of
Burgun, Schverer & Co.**
**1. Is the form relatively simple, and perhaps raised upon
solid, circular feet?**
2. Is the subject floral?
3. Is the piece signed?
4. Has use been made of internal mottling?
5. Is the piece hand-carved?
6. Is the decoration fire-polished or martelé-cut?
**7. Does the piece feature a wide range of colours
(including gilding)?**

**Burgun, Schverer & Co.
(French, 1711-present)**
Following the Franco-Prussian
War (1870-71), the previously
French provinces of Alsace and
Lorraine were annexed by
Germany, and the long-
established Lorraine glassmaking
firm of Burgun, Schverer & Co.
found itself in Germany.
However, the firm maintained its
contacts with France, and
particularly with Emile Gallé (see
pp.46-9), who had served a
three-year apprenticeship at the
firm's factory at Meisenthal
during the late 1860s. In 1885,
Burgun, Schverer & Co. entered
into a contract to produce glass
for Emile Gallé. Also in that
year, the designer Desiré

Christian joined the firm (see
opposite). The firm also designed
a few one-off pieces to
commission. Today Burgun,
Schverer & Co. is back in
France, operating as Verrerie de
Meisanthal.

Characteristics
Burgun, Schverer & Co. were
the only German company to
produce cameo glass during this
early period. Forms tended to be
conservative and included
traditional Venetian and
naturalistic-inspired examples.
The emphasis was on decoration,
which was influenced by local
flora such as cowparsley, and the
thistle (the emblem of Lorraine),
which figures on the vase in the

main picture. Pieces were fire-polished and surfaces generally feature martelé (planished) surface decoration. Bases tend to be solid, and silver mounts were used on some examples.

* Other decorative techniques used by Burgun, Schverer & Co. at the time included acid-cutting (see *below*), foil inclusions, gilding and the use of overlay.

* Some pieces, known as *vases parlantes*, include amongst the decoration inscribed verses in French, a technique also used by Gallé.

Marks

Wares are marked with an etched gilt thistle and cross of Lorraine, accompanied by the words "VERRERIE D'ART DE LORRAINE BS & CO", or a variation on these three elements. Some Burgun, Schverer & Co. wares from before c.1870 bear Gallé's signature as well.

Desiré Christian (French, born 1846)

Christian was Burgun, Schverer & Co.'s chief artistic designer until 1896, when he opened his own firm, initially called Christian Frères et Fils, with his brother François and son Armand. Christian excelled in vases with enamelled decoration encased within a further layer of clear glass. He often cut away the outer surface to reveal the layer of colour beneath. Examples of his work also display isolated surface carving, usually upon thick-walled vases, with colourful internal and surface streaking.

The enamelled coupe *above* is typical of the firm's Art Nouveau acid-cut pieces: a design was etched onto a piece coated with wax, which was then dipped in acid to cut out the design. Craftsmen often applied gilding and enamelling in conjunction with cameo and internal decoration. Such pieces usually reflect styles and motifs from Ancient Egypt or, as in this case, Renaissance Venice, and cannot be called pure Art Nouveau.

This etched, polished and applied green vase, *above*, produced by Christian's firm, is very similar to the wares designed under Christian at Burgun, Schverer & Co. It has tear-drop appliqués around the neck.

It is not known exactly which pieces were designed by Christian himself, and which were designed by his brother, his son, or one of the firm's other designers, although a small number are engraved with the monogram "D.Ch." In general, wares carry the signature of the firm "DESIRE CHRISTIAN".

EMILE GALLÉ: 1

An intaglio-carved verrerie parlante *designed by Emile Gallé c.1904; ht 4½in/11cm; value code A*

Identification checklist for Gallé's studio glassware
1. Is the piece clearly hand-made and hand-decorated?
2. Is it sculptural in appearance?
3. Is the form nonconformist or unusual?
4. Is the piece signed on the base, or on the side, perhaps with a cross of Lorraine?
5. Are decorative motifs inspired by floral subjects or insect-life, or if enamelled, Iznik-inspired?
6. Is the piece carved?
7. Is the body embellished with applied naturalistic forms such as flora, molluscs, crustacea or mushrooms?
8. Is any use made of *marqueterie de verre* (see *opposite*)?
9. Is the piece a *verrerie parlante* (see *opposite*)?

Identification checklist for Gallé's cameo glassware
1. Is the piece constructed of two or more layers of glass?
2. Is it fire-polished or martelé-carved (see p.48)?
3. Does it have a carved signature, with perhaps a star motif?
4. Is the base solid and of one colour?
5. Does the underside exhibit a pontil mark?

Emile Gallé (French, 1846-1904)
Born in Nancy in Lorraine, Emile Gallé was considered the greatest master-craftsman in glass, even within his own lifetime. The workshop that he founded in 1874 produced both ceramics and glass, but it is as a glass artist that Gallé is best known. He realised the sculptural potential of the medium, and managed to capture in glass the sense of movement

so desired by exponents of Art Nouveau. In his search for a new approach to modelling glass, Gallé invented several new glassmaking techniques, such as *marquetrie de verre* (see *below*), and worked constantly to develop other methods. Many of his pieces combine a number of techniques.

Gallé's early wares

Initially, Gallé produced hand-finished and -decorated wares in green- or brown-tinted or clear glass, moulded into innovative forms, and carved, sometimes with an incised or sunken decoration called intaglio carving, like that, *left*. Decoration often depicts floral subjects or insects.

The glass body of the ewer *above* is carved with dragonfly wings and blossoms, with the handle formed as the dragonfly's body. The foot of the ewer is carved with tadpoles. The typically clear glass body is striated with dark blue, a process adopted by Gallé c.1895. The dragonfly's body is enamelled in rust and black; much of Gallé's earlier work incorporated enamelled decoration. The dragonfly's body is also gilded, a common feature of Gallé's enamelled glasswares.
* Some of Gallé's enamelled glass is decorated with bold Japanese or Islamic patterns, the latter inspired by Syrian glassware produced around Damascus during the 13th and 14thC.
* Enamelled wares may have a painted gilt or black, or occasionally a carved signature on the base.

Later studio wares

From 1889, Gallé concentrated on producing the innovative wares for which he is best known. Pieces took more sculptural forms and Gallé made greater use of mottled and striated glass, and of naturalistic decoration. Many pieces are decorated using the traditional *marquetrie de verre* process, invented by Gallé, whereby pieces of hot coloured glass are pressed into the hot and malleable body of a vessel and then rolled in. Once cool, the glass is then carved on a wheel. Other pieces are intaglio carved, and some bear an engraved verse, generally by Victor Prouvé, Mallarmé, Baudelaire or other French giants of literature; these are referred to as *verreries parlantes*, or speaking vases.
* Studio glassware is hand-made and likely to have been produced either as unique pieces or in very limited editions, and is therefore particularly valuable.

Much Gallé glassware has applied decoration, commonly floral; the vase *above*, called *L'orchidee*, is applied with an orchid flower. Crustacea, molluscs and mushrooms are also found, but are rare and hence particularly sought by collectors.

From 1900, the firm used mass-production techniques, particularly in the production of cameo glass (see pp.48-9). Production of the more exclusive studio glass continued, in conjunction with industrially produced wares, until Gallé's death. His studio wares are not dated, but are clearly hand-finished and show none of the signs of mechanisation that characterize his later work.

EMILE GALLÉ: 2

Gallé cameo glassware

Cameo glasswares, constructed
using two or more coloured layers
of glass from which decoration is
cut or carved away, were the
staple product of the Gallé
glassworks. At first hand-made,
the later cameo glass (made after
c.1904) was almost invariably
industrially made (see *right*).

Gallé's hand carving is noticeably
deeper than on machine-made
pieces. This coupe on a stand,
above, is hand-carved, which adds
a premium to its value. The
design of the five-pronged base,
with each prong set with a carved
cicada, is highly innovative. The
foil inclusions used to highlight
the wings and eyes of the cicadas
would not be found on the
industrially carved pieces. Hand-
carved pieces tend to be fire-
polished, and also exhibit
martelé cutting; this coupe has
been splashed with colour and
then polished. The light amber
mottling here is particularly
unusual.

**Industrially produced cameo
wares**

From 1899, with the help of
increased mechanisation, Gallé
began to produce cameo glass on
a commercial scale. These later
works realised the potential of
glass to sheer plasticity, thus
providing a perfect medium for
the Art Nouveau approach, and
are the most usual type of Gallé
cameo glass found today. In
response to enormous advance-
ments in the novel phenomenon
of electricity, a certain proportion
of these industrially made wares
consisted of lamps.

The functional aspect of the
lamp *above* enhances the
decorative: the light illuminates
the stem and the waterfall that
runs its length. This lamp is
three-coloured, but four- and
five-layer examples exist; the
more layers, the more desirable
the piece.

* Always check for damage: the
top should be removed and the
metal mount that fixes onto the
top of the base, to hold the bulb
into the shade and into the stem,
examined. Heat can cause the
glass to crack and damage may be
obscured by the metal collar.
Damage to bases, which are
usually of a single colour, can be
repaired with hand-coloured resin.

The vase *above* is made of a form
of mould-blown glass called
"blowout" glass. This example
has been wheel-carved with cala
lilies and contains four layers of

glass – blue, white, mauve and green. The base is, typically, of a single colour. Being mould-blown, these popular vase types could be produced in comparatively large numbers and are thus relatively common. The strong colouring of this piece makes it particularly desirable – an almost identical vase in plum, brown and yellow would not attract as high a price.

Gallé produced a number of *veilleuses*, or nightlights, with sculptural metal mounts. The example *above* is supported by three dragonflies in silvered bronze; the spherical amber glass shade is etched with oak leaves and acorns that echo the leaf-form feet of the dragonflies. Other mounts may reflect the decorative theme of the shade.

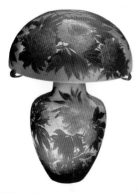

This table lamp, *above*, is one of the most striking and desirable examples of Gallé's work. The vibrant peony decoration is intricately etched, with great

attention given to the detailing of the flowerheads. This gives the lamp a strong sense of depth, particularly when illuminated from behind. Its great size makes this one of the most expensive of the industrially made examples. The shade and stem exhibit "blowout" decoration, which further enhances the value.
* The combination of red and yellow was particularly popular.
* Lamps of this type and similar examples with wisteria decoration have been particularly sought after by Japanese dealers and collectors during the past few years.

The landscape vase *above* is of the type most common today. The decoration is stiffer, with shallower carving, although this does have the advantage of allowing the internal yellow mottling to show through as a part of the design. Careful carving and the depth of the purple glass layer have allowed toning from light mauve to almost black.
* Gallé's cameo landscape vases generally fetch higher prices than those with the floral decoration. Other subjects include polar bears, elephants and fish, but landscapes and flora predominate.

Dating and marks

Emile Gallé marked his pieces with a wide variety of cameo and incise-carved signatures. For three years following his death, a star was added after and slightly above the signature, which is traditionally held to represent the loss of France's shining star. After 1907 the firm reverted to using Gallé's signature.

DAUM FRÈRES

A Daum table lamp and shade
1900; ht 19in/48.5cm; value code A

Identification checklist for the glasswares designed by the Daum brothers
1. Is the piece relatively sculptural?
2. Is it carved, enamelled or cameo-carved (see *opposite*)?
3. Is the carving delicately executed?
4. Does decoration feature natural (rather than figural) motifs?
5. Has use been made of mottled decoration?
6. Is there any enamelling?
7. Is the piece signed?
8. Does the design disappear over the edge of the piece?
9. Is the base carved?

Daum Frères (French, 1875-present)
The Daum brothers, Auguste (1853-1909) and Antonin (1864-1930), worked with Emile Gallé (see pp.46-9) before establishing their own glassworks in Nancy. No distinction has so far been made between their work. Like other members of the Nancy School, their early products were inspired by the flora and fauna of their native Lorraine. The firm produced technically competent and innovative vases and lamps of high quality. Most were sculptural in form with mottled decoration and distinctively delicate carving. The table lamp in the main picture, made in overlaid and etched glass, is typical of their Art Nouveau

wares, most of which were produced before 1914. The firm went on to produce heavy, acid-cut pieces, often with geometric decoration, and still operates today as Cristallerie Daum.

Cameo glass

Although Daum produced some carved and enamelled pieces, most of their Art Nouveau wares are cameo glass or acid-cut and colour-enamelled. A rare technique was intercalaire: pieces would be cameo-carved – usually by laminating two layers of glass together – and then covered with a layer of carved or etched semi-transparent glass.

The use of underlying mottling to provide toning is evident on this tall rainstorm vase, *above*. The factory produced a number of similar pieces with autumnal and winter scenes, and those displaying the rain-streaked effect evident on this piece are particularly sought-after. The firm was also adept at enamelling on top of carved decoration: the green on the base of this vase has been painted onto carving. The

enamelled tree is typical of Daum in that it disappears over the edge of the vase. Beware of cut-down vases with irregular rims, sharp edges and a polished appearance.

Decoration is sometimes picked out with gilt, as in the handled vase shown *above*. This has a mottled ground with a carved surface.
* Vase bases are sometimes shallow, and carved with stylized bands on a granular background.
* Some pieces feature metal mounts by Louis Majorelle (see pp.14-5).
* Figural decoration is rare.
* On mould-blown or "blowout" vases, where the glass was blown into a mould, the design appears in relief over a mottled ground. The mould lines are visible, but should not be too pronounced.
* The applied glass snails on the lamp increase the desirability of the piece, and may add as much as 40% to the value.

Collecting point

Daum glass divides into the popular sculptural and other technically complicated studio work, and the industrially produced (though still hand-carved) pieces. Despite being industrially made, all the pieces shown here are of high quality and would command high prices.

Marks

These appear in several forms. Some pieces are signed in cameo, but most feature the gilt signature, "DAUM, NANCY", on black enamel on the underside of the base. The signature appears with the cross of Lorraine.

MÜLLER FRÈRES

A rare cameo glass vase with Japanese decoration by Müller Frères c.1900; ht 16½in/42cm; value code A/B

Identification checklist for Müller Frères' cameo glass wares
1. Is the glass internally mottled or streaked?
2. Is any floral detail well-carved, with attention given to depth and perspective?
3. Is the piece signed in cameo?
4. Is the form of relatively standard type?
5. If a vase, does it have a short, everted neck?
6. Does the piece bear the firm's mark?

Müller Frères (French, active c.1900-1933)
Henri and Desiré Müller worked initially with Emile Gallé (see pp.46-9). In 1895, Henri Müller set up a workshop in Lunéville, near Nancy, where he was later joined by Desiré and others. Their glassware was blown at

their Croismare factory before being sent to Lunéville for decoration. Except for a brief period of closure in 1914, the business prospered until it was disbanded.

The Müller brothers worked in a variety of styles, but are best known for their industrially produced cameo glassware. Many designs ape those popularized by Gallé. They were particularly proficient with floral and landscape decoration applied to vases, ceiling bowls and table lamps. Some of their rarer work includes Japanese-inspired decoration: the vase in the main picture features stylized landscapes, figures and birds.

Cameo decoration

In cameo decoration, two pieces of glass, usually of contrasting colours, are superimposed, and a design ground into the upper layer (see p.64). Müller cameo wares were often fire-polished. The glass body would be left matt, or with a satin surface.

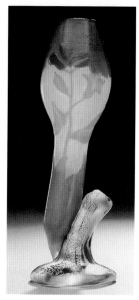

Müller's rarest wares are the sculptural studio pieces, which tend to have overlaid, carved and internal decoration. The fire-polished lily vase, *above*, is overlaid in lavender, white and lime green. The stem is decorated inside with foil.

Marks

Pieces are marked either "Müller Frères – Lunéville" or "Müller-Croismare", or simply "M.F". Most acid-etched glass was made at Lunéville, whilst wheel-carved pieces came from Croismare.

LÉGRAS (French, 1864-present)

The work of Auguste Légras bears a strong resemblance to that of Gallé, Daum and Müller Frères, but generally commands lower prices. He made enamelled cameo vases and commercial glassware, including perfume bottles designed by Lalique.

Légras preferred mainly floral and landscape decoration, as in the enamelled glass lamp, *above*, which resembles Daum's woodlands. The effect of fire-polishing is visible on relief areas.
* Légras favoured internally mottled or streaked glass.
* His pieces are usually signed "LÉGRAS".

A word of advice

If a lamp has a collar mount, this should be removed and the neck beneath checked. If it is encased in metal, examine the glass carefully for signs of stress cracks (see p.48).

Lamps could be lit internally, with one light for the shade and one for the base. Avoid pieces where the base has been drilled to take a wire. Usually, the stems of such lamps were hollow, and the wire went under the lamp. A recess for the wire prevented the lamp from wobbling.

ALMÉRIC WALTER

A group of pâte-de-verre *wares produced by Alméric Walter
left, centre c.1910; right c.1920; value code B/C each*

**Identification checklist for glasswares produced by
Alméric Walter**

1. Is the piece *pâte-de-verre* (see *below*)?
2. Does it make use of opaque and, in some areas,
partially translucent glass?
3. Is it heavy in weight?
4. Does it make use of naturalistic decorative elements,
such as reptiles modelled in high relief?
5. Is it marked with the intaglio-moulded signature of the
firm (see *facing page*)?
6. Does it bear the impress-moulded signature of the
designer?
7. Does the surface appear waxed?
8. Is the base ground flat?

**Alméric Walter (French,
1859-1942)**
Walter was primarily a
manufacturer of glasswares,
rather than a designer. From
c.1906 to 1914 he operated a
workshop in Nancy for the Daum
brothers (see pp.50-1), which
specialized in the production of
bibelots, paperweights and small
dishes in *pâte-de-verre* ("glass

paste"). In 1919, Walter set up
his own factory, which remained
in production into the 1920s.

Pâte-de-verre
The Daum factory was the first
firm to exploit *pâte-de-verre* on a
commercial basis. The ancient
technique involves the use of
coloured glass powder mixed
with a liquid to form a paste.

The paste is packed into a reusable mould. Multi-coloured pieces can be created by packing different pastes on top of one another. When placed in a kiln and fired at the critical temperature, the glass fuses rather than melts. Walter was one of the foremost French masters of the *pâte-de-verre* method of the Art Nouveau period, along with Albert Damousse (1848-1926) and Henri Cros (see *below*).

Range and decoration
The Walter factory produced mainly small, useful wares, as well as covered boxes. Their use of the *pâte-de-verre* technique reached a high point with a series of highly detailed, densely speckled salamanders and chameleons. Walter's modellers included Henri Bergé, who specialized in insects, reptiles and fish, and modelled all the pieces in the main picture except the dish on the right. Another modeller, Alfred Finot, created small nudes. Finot's work is rarer than that of Bergé.
* The Walter modellers often contrasted blues and yellows.

Marks
Most Walter products made after 1919 bear the moulded signature, "A. WALTER NANCY", as well as the impressed signature of the designer. Pieces designed by Walter before 1914 are marked "DAUM NANCY".
* Copies or fakes are not known.

HENRI CROS (French, 1840-1907)
From 1891 the Sèvres porcelain factory (see pp.78-9) put a workshop at the disposal of Henri Cros, one of the modern progenitors of the *pâte-de-verre* process. He designed a series of *pâte-de-verre* plaques with relief decoration, inspired by ancient wares exhibited in Paris in 1878; these tend to have a strongly sculptural feel, and a maquette-type appearance. Some are dated. Because the glass paste was not easily controlled, it can contain a multitude of internal fissures, and surfaces may feel granular or sugary. Colour tends to be streaked and uneven.

Cros's work tends to be fairly small-scale, and decorated with classical portraits.

Cros figures, like the bust of a woman *above*, may be modelled in high relief, or as profiles in low relief.

Marks
Some pieces designed by Henri Cros are impressed with the name, "CROS", in capital letters.
* Plaques sometimes bear the month and year of production.

LOETZ

A large Loetz vase
c.1900; ht 10½in/26cm; value code C

Identification checklist for the iridescent glasswares produced by Loetz

1. Is the piece covered with controlled iridescence?
2. Is the glass body solid and relatively thick?
3. Is the piece marked?
4. Is the form inventive?
5. Is the glass body of purple or amber colour?
6. Does the decoration display a spectrum of colours?
7. Are any handles slender and sinuous?
8. Does the piece feature any silver casing?

Loetz (Austrian, 1836-1939)
This glassmaking firm, founded at Klostermühle by Johann Loetz, specialized in making high-quality art glass. The firm was known as Glasfabrik Johann-Loetz Witwe after 1848, when Loetz died and his widow Suzanne took over direction, and was guided to success by Max von Spaun, the designer who introduced the iridescent glasswares that attracted attention during the 1880s and for which the firm won numerous awards. Loetz took the Art Nouveau spirit to heart and their iridescent wares combine finely controlled surface decoration with highly inventive glass forms. At the Vienna Jubilee Exhibition of 1898, Loetz showed a group of iridescent wares which soon rivalled the products of Louis Comfort Tiffany in popularity. Although many collectors view Loetz glass as the Austrian attempt to emulate Tiffany, it was actually Tiffany who was impressed by the Loetz wares shown at the various international exhibitions. In fact, many Loetz creations predate similar works by Tiffany. Loetz also produced cameo wares, but these are fairly rare.

Decoration

The thick, solid body of Loetz iridescent wares is sometimes a dark colour. Those with deep purple bodies, highlighted with silver and peacock blue iridescence, were very popular during the period and are the most collectable today. Wares in dark amber glass with green-gold iridescence are also very popular. The colour of the vase in the main picture is unusual, but the controlled, feathered decoration, iridescent gold motifs and slender handles are typical. Loetz also pioneered the use of electrolytic deposit techniques. The most desirable of such pieces are those with a distinctively Art Nouveau design, usually with stylized flowerheads upon scrolling or whiplash stems.

Forms

Loetz forms are very inventive, and sometimes recall Persian or Roman models. Pieces often make use of applied handles (see main picture), usually in slender shapes trailing from or around the body piece.

This "goose-neck" vase is based on a Turkish rosewater sprinkler. Other vases have straight necks, without the swollen knop, or resemble "Jack in the Pulpit" vases (see pp. 72-3). Pontils are ground, except on pieces with metal frames, which usually have moulded bases.

One of the most famous sculptors associated with the company, Gustav Gurschner (see pp. 126-7), produced a memorable series of table lamps. The example shown, *above*, is very much in his style, although it is not signed. Gurschner often used stylized female forms or flowerheads, as in this example.
* The feathering on the shade of this piece is typical.

Other wares

Loetz also produced glass in contrasting primary colours, as well as a variety of lamp shades for Koloman Moser (see p. 60-1). From c.1900, Loetz made large quantities of "Papillon" (Butterfly) glass, decorated with closely clustered iridescent peacock or kingfisher blue raindrop splashes.
* Another Loetz designer, Michael Powolny, used vibrant colours, such as orange and yellow combined, with applied black rims and decoration.

Marks

Items made for export are marked "LOETZ" or "LOETZ AUSTRIA". Other wares may carry engraved crossed arrows, or are unmarked.

E. BAKALOWITS & SÖHNE

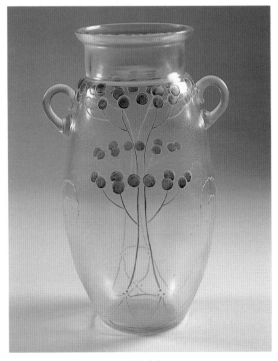

*A two-handled Bakalowits vase
1905; ht approx. 8in/20cm; value code F*

Identification checklist for the glasswares of Bakalowits
1. Is the piece relatively lightweight and fairly thinly walled?
2. Is the glass of pale green lustre?
3. Does it have a satin iridescent surface?
4. If enamelled, is the decoration organic or floral?
5. Is the base moulded, with no sign of a pontil mark?
6. Is the shape avant-garde, although loosely based on a classical form?

**E. Bakalowits & Söhne
(Austrian, established 1845)**
One of the leading Austrian retailers of glassware at the beginning of the 20thC was the Viennese firm of Bakalowits. With the rise in popularity of iridescent glass, the firm commissioned a number of striking avant-garde pieces from such leading designers as Koloman Moser of the Wiener

Werkstätte (see pp.60-1).

The pearlized, iridescent surface of wares such as the pale green vase in the main picture has led many people to regard them as insubstantial competition for the bolder, more colourful designs of Loetz (see pp.56-7), and indeed, Bakalowits products are sometimes wrongly catalogued as Loetz, although they are typically thinner and less

substantial, with less pronounced iridescence. Also, Bakalowits wares tend to have moulded bases, without a visible pontil mark. Recently, Bakalowits wares have begun to be appreciated in their own right, although they will probably never achieve the desirability of Loetz.
* Bakalowits wares are unmarked.
* Designs tend to be symmetrical, often with stylized floral decoration.
* Many pieces make use of silver mounts.

A distinctive feature of Palme-König wares is the use of trailed spider's web-type decoration, as on the vase *above*. Decoration typically uses light-coloured overlays against dark grounds, such as claret or the green on this piece. On frosted pieces, the process was reversed, with dark trailing on a light ground.
* The iridescent surface is less controlled than on Loetz pieces.

This electroplate-mounted glass sherry jug, *above*, designed by Koloman Moser, shows Bakalowits producing to the order of a designer rather than for a commercial range. This piece would probably fetch many times the price of the vase in the main picture, by virtue of its association with Moser.
* Although information on Bakalowits is scanty, in recent years a number of exhibitions have shown the firm's glass wares. Documentation exists for Moser's work.

The decoration of the iridescent vase, *above*, produced at Palme-König c.1900, has a random, splattered effect. Like those of Bakalowits, Palme-König iridescent pieces are often wrongly attributed to Loetz, but they lack the level of control usually evident on Loetz glass.

PALME-KÖNIG (Bohemian, established 1786)

The Bohemian commercial glassmakers Palme-König produced good-quality Art Nouveau iridescent glasswares and table glass. The firm employed forms pioneered by Loetz, with the result that its work is often seen as a less expensive imitation of Loetz.

Identification

Palme-König wares, mainly vases and bowls under 12in (30.5cm) high, are not marked. The most common colours are green, amethyst and deep red. Bases are often moulded; the iridescent vase is unusual in having a ground pontil mark. Beware of spurious Loetz marks.

THE WIENER WERKSTÄTTE

*A Wiener Werkstätte glass table lamp designed by Otto Prutscher
1908; ht 15in/38cm; value code B/C*

Identification checklist for glasswares designed by Otto Prutscher for the Wiener Werkstätte
1. If a glass, is the stem very thin?
2. Is the glass clear, but overlaid with decoration (usually in one colour)?
3. Are decorative motifs geometrical?
4. Is there any chequered decoration?
5. Is the bowl as large (or larger) than the foot?

Wiener Werkstätte glasswares
The members of the Wiener Werkstätte, or Vienna Workshops (see pp.22-3), produced designs for glasswares in a variety of styles. The most important designs were by Josef Hoffmann, Koloman Moser, Dagobert Pèche and Otto Prutscher. Prominent glassmakers, such as Loetz (see pp.56-7) and Lobmeyr made the Wiener Werkstätte designs. Hoffmann and Prutscher's designs were made by the firm of Meyr's Neffe.
* For the collector, it is more important to know the designer of a particular piece, than which firm was responsible for its execution.

Otto Prutscher (Austrian, 1880-1949)

Although best known for his jewelry and silver, Prutscher designed some of the Wiener Werkstätte's most distinctive glasswares. He used a traditional Austrian and Bohemian form of glass decoration in which glass was flashed with a single colour and then carved and polished to form a design pattern. Prutscher adapted this technique to produce unique pieces that were strongly geometric both in form and in decoration. The clear glass table lamp shown in the main picture is a typical example of his technique. In addition to table lamps, Prutscher produced various suites of glassware flashed in a wide range of colours. Those pieces with stronger colours are the most desirable.
* Prutscher's designs are collectable singly.

Moser's glasswares

The designs produced by Koloman Moser were executed by Bakalowits (see pp.58-9) and by Loetz (who also manufactured glasswares designed by Michael Powolny, see pp.56-7).

Moser's designs were revolutionary and differed radically from Loetz's more usual iridescent wares. As shown by the bowl *above*, his designs were acid-cut on overlay and embellished with enamelling. The use of ball feet is characteristic of his work (see pp.22-3 and 138-9).

Other designers

Until the 1920s, Josef Hoffmann's glass designs concentrated on decorative form. He often used flutes. Maria Kirschner designed vases of unusual shape, executed in iridescent glass by Loetz.

The chequered motif on the stem of this rose-pink wine glass, *above*, is almost Prutscher's trademark. The dangerously long, thin stem of this piece is also typical of his work. For stability, glassmakers invariably prefer the foot to be wider than the rest of the piece. However, Prutscher produced many pieces like this, where the bowl is as large, or larger than, the foot.
* The condition of such delicate pieces is all-important.

During the Art Nouveau period, some glassware was produced from designs by Austrian art students. Alternatively, the design of a well-known member of the Wiener Werkstätte was executed by a *Fachschüle* (art college). The *bonbonnière above*, with alternating clear and enamelled bands, was produced by Fachschüle Haida to a design by Karl Pohl. Some pieces have a signature or maker's name inscribed in gilt on the base.

A Whitefriars centrepiece, probably designed by Harry Powell c.1906; ht 14in/36cm; value code D

Identification checklist for James Powell & Sons glass
1. Is the piece made of clear or olive green glass or, alternatively, opalescent glass, perhaps toning from pale turquoise to opaque white ?
2. Is the form fairly unconventional, perhaps with a crimped rim?
3. Does decoration involve trailing in emerald green?
4. Is the piece marked?
5. Is it delicate looking?
6. Is it thinly-walled?

James Powell & Sons (English, c.1834-1980)
James Powell & Sons was established in London where during the latter part of the 19thC they produced a range of decorative glasswares such as lampshades, tablewares and paperweights. Among the firm's Art Nouveau glasswares were vases with furnace-wrought decoration, sometimes with trailed emerald green feathering, evident on the centrepiece in the main picture, or with gold aventurine in knopped stems. The example shown in the main picture, *above*, was actually produced by Whitefriars Glass Works, a London glassworks founded c.1680 and bought by James Powell in 1834. The use of enamelwork makes this a particularly valuable piece.

Designers employed by Powell included the architects Philip Webb and Sir T. G. Jackson, and Harry J. Powell (see *below*).

Some Powell wares were produced in an opalescent glass shading from pale turquoise to opaque bluish white, called "straw opaline" because it shows a brownish tinge when held to the light. Other pieces were made in pale green soda glass which lacks the sharp "ring" of lead glass.

In the 1890's Powell produced a range of clear vases with floral engraving in an Art Nouveau style designed by Heywood Sumner. The firm also made glass inclusions for other peoples' wares – for example, for the light fittings designed by W. A. S. Benson, and the green glass mounts used in Tudric pewter, Cymric silver, and for the silver-mounted wares of Ashbee's Guild of Handicraft.

Many of Powell's glass and decanter shapes were inspired by glass depicted in Old Master paintings, or by 16thC Venetian forms – clearly the inspiration for this green-tinted decanter of 1908. The decoration is typically simple.

Harry J. Powell (English, 1853-1922)
Harry Powell controlled James Powell & Sons between 1880 and 1914. Under his direction, the firm produced green glass wares with silver mounts, inspired by the Arts and Crafts movement.

Marks
The glass is unmarked but often the silver component of Powell's wares is stamped with the initials "JPS", *below*.

JAMES COUPER & SONS (Scottish, dates unknown)
James Couper & Sons is best known for its "Clutha" glass, which was developed c.1885 and remained in production until c.1905. Clutha glass tends to be a cloudy yellow, green, amber or pink with variegated bubbles and streaks. The range included decorative wares, vases, bottles and tablewares. Shapes were often based on antique Roman and Islamic models.

Early Clutha designs were by Christopher Dresser (1834-1904), the celebrated industrial designer. Much of it was sold by Liberty's and bears the mark "CLUTHA REGD. DESIGNED BY C.D." in a circle surrounding Liberty's "lotus" trademark.

The other prominent designer at James Couper & Sons was George Walton (1867-1933), who concentrated on using green-tinted glass, sometimes randomly speckled with small particles of gold, copper or some other metal, known as aventurine: this bowl is typical of his wares.
* It is generally difficult to distinguish the styles of Dresser and Walton, although the latter's forms were generally the more restrained. The Walton pieces are not marked.
* It has long been accepted that "clutha" meant "cloudy" in Old Scottish, but it is also said to be the Gaelic name for the River Clyde.

STOURBRIDGE

*An overlay glass vase by Thomas Webb & Sons
1900; ht 6¾in/17cm; value code F*

Identification checklist for Webb's overlay glass
1. Is the overlay of a single colour?
2. Is any surface decoration carved, rather than in relief?
3. Does the piece display the prismatic effect achieved by martelé cutting (see *opposite*)?
4. Is the martelé cutting broad?
5. Is there a cameo signature?
6. Is the piece a vase?

Stourbridge

In the 17thC a group of immigrant glassworkers from Lorraine settled in Stourbridge, in the English Midlands, and established a glassmaking centre. Firms such as Richardson & Sons, Brierley Hill, Thomas Webb & Sons (see *below*) and Stevens & Williams (see *opposite*) developed a reputation for fine, unusual and often extremely innovative glasswares.

Thomas Webb & Sons (1856-present)

Thomas Webb's glassworks at Stourbridge began producing fine quality wares in 1856. The firm's earliest examples of Art Nouveau-type design was a range of heavily gilded Burmese ware vases (see p.176), influenced by Japanese design. The firm is best known for "rock crystal", cameo wares and overlay glass.

Cameo glass

Cameo glass was first developed by the Romans and revived in England in the mid-19thC. The process, whereby two or more layers of glass, often of varying colours, are laminated together, then carved on a wheel or etched to make a design in high relief, was perfected at Webb during the Victorian period by the Woodall brothers, George (1850-1925) and Thomas (1849-1926), and production continued into the Art Nouveau period. Another important exponent of cameo glass was Emile Gallé (see p.48).

Overlay glass

Webb's most important contribution to Art Nouveau was their overlay glass, although it never achieved the popularity of the cameo glass and hence was made in smaller numbers. Overlay, or cased glass, is similar to cameo glass, but with the design on the outer layer upon an underlying clear glass form. The overlay process was more industrial than the intricate carving of the cameo process, and therefore simpler. Webb's overlay wares are not as sophisticated as their cameo glass. The overlay vase in the main picture is a poor fusion of form and decoration, which might be considered stiff or even clumsy. The prismatic effect is achieved by broad martelé cutting, a distinctive feature of much of Webb's overlay glass. This piece was first mould-blown, then wheel-cut and fire-polished. Variations of this type exist, some overlaid with green glass rather than blue, and some with a top rim lined with blue overlay. Others, instead of the prism-cut surface shown here, have a semi-frosted craquelure effect achieved by acid-cutting.

Marks

Most Webb wares bear one of the marks *below*, etched or printed. Their cameo glass was etched with "THOMAS WEBB & SONS". Rock crystal wares are stencilled with either "Webb" or, on later pieces, "Webb, England".

Stevens & Williams (English, c.1830-present)

This Stourbridge firm is most noted for the cameo wares of Joshua Hodgetts (1858-1933) and John Northwood (1837-1902), and the engraved rock crystal wares produced by Joseph Keller. Today, the firm operates under the name Brierly Royal Crystal.

Flashed glasswares

The flashing process, whereby the surface of the glass is applied with a thin glass plating, usually in a stronger colour, became widespread in 19thC England as an inexpensive way to produce parti-coloured glassware. Stevens & Williams's flashed wares tend to have more inventive forms than their overlay counterparts, and often have finely executed carved decoration. Similarly, decoration and form are generally better harmonized on flashed wares than on the overlay pieces.

Marks

Some Stevens & Williams wares bear the firm's name or initials etched or impressed. Individual designers did not sign their wares.

The red and yellow vase *above* was marketed as "alexandrite", after the greenish-brown gemstone that seems to change to red or reddish-brown in certain light. Lalique (see pp.130-1) produced some moulded glasswares with this name, which changed colour when transferred from natural to artificial light. However, despite its name, the vase shown here does not have this quality.

The fine cutting of the flashed vase *above* is typical of Stevens & Williams, as is the safe shape. The Art Nouveau feel is created by the floral and whiplash motifs.

An Apple Blossom *leaded glass and bronze Tiffany table lamp c.1910; ht 27in/68.5cm, shade dia. 18in/45.5cm; value code A*

Identification checklist for Tiffany lamps

1. Are the base and stem bronze or gilt bronze?
2. Is the base stamped "Tiffany Studios New York" and numbered?
3. Is the shade marked with an applied bronze pad?
4. Does the base complement the shade in form and perhaps also in decorative motif?
5. Are the individual pieces of glass set in a bronze framework?
6. Is the shade multi-coloured?
7. Does it incorporate floral, dragonfly, bamboo or zodiacal motifs, or Renaissance or medieval motifs?
8. Is the glass streaked and opaque?

Tiffany Studios (American, 1879-1936)
Louis Comfort, son of the renowned American jeweler, Charles Tiffany, founded Louis C. Tiffany & Associated Artists which became Tiffany Studios. In 1900 the firm designed interiors for private and public buildings, such as the White House in Washington. Tiffany's unique style became a driving force behind the emergent Art Nouveau style. In 1880, he patented an iridescent glass called favrile (meaning hand-

made), which became their staple material, and the type most often found today. Louis Comfort became art director of his father's company, Tiffany and Co., in 1902.

Tiffany's lamps

Tiffany table lamps were made in two sections; the base and stem, and the shade. Shades consist of many pieces of favrile glass set in a bronze framework of irregular lozenge shapes, with decoration often inspired by organic and naturalistic motifs. Dragonflies are common, as are Renaissance, zodiacal and medieval motifs. Bases are bronze or gilt bronze, and sometimes incorporate tilework or mosaicwork. The shade can reflect the design: the irregular border of the example in the main picture enhances the organic effect of the tree-like base and floral motifs.
* Similar lamps were also made in standard and ceiling form.
* Shades are sometimes crimped to resemble silk; others have pierced bronze bases with glass blown into the frames.
* Larger leaded shades may have supporting struts on the interior.
* Being hand-made, no two shades are alike although they may be made to the same design.

Many lamps have complementary bases and shades, but it is unusual for these elements to be integral, as they are in the *Zinnia* lamp, *above*, inlaid with leaded and mosaic glass to imitate zinnias. The base is designed as six trees supporting the shade. This was probably a one-off and is thus particularly desirable, as most Tiffany pieces were made in editions of more than one.
* If integral elements are separated, a piece will lose value.

The pond lily lamp *above*, the most successful of the non-leaded glass types, is typical in being of a single colour using favrile glass flowerhead shades.

Fakes and copies

Fakes and copies abound. Some incorporate original wiring and genuine Tiffany glass, which fell into unscrupulous hands in the 1960s. Fakes may have convincing marks, but forgers often overlook the small pad found on most genuine shades.

The six-dragonfly lamp *above* is the most common of several versions in which details vary. Some include coloured glass cabochons, either pitted around the shade or used for eyes, as here. These insects' heads are contained by the shade, but some "drophead" dragonflies protrude beyond the rim. The wings are of pierced grille laid over the glass.

TIFFANY STUDIOS: 2

As well as table lamps and lampshades (see previous pages), Louis Comfort Tiffany produced vases and scent bottles, tiles, lamps, stained-glass windows and glass mosaics, both ecclesiastical and secular, and desk furniture. Some mosaics measure as much as 15 × 49ft (4.6 × 15m).

Tiffany developed and used innovative glassmaking methods. He avoided surface decoration, preferring to make ornament integral to the body of the piece. However, he was a designer of glassware rather than a maker, and paid little heed to the technical aspect of working in glass and the craftsmen employed at the factory to produce his designs often found them technically impossible. For every hundred or so attempts, only one design might prove practical. To achieve the natural agate effect on the vase pictured *below* requires great technical expertise.

Towards the end of the 19thC, ancient glass was found around the Mediterranean. Generally of Roman origin, the glass had developed a beautiful iridescent surface, as the result of being buried. Tiffany's ''Cypriote'' wares, like the vase *above*, from c.1895, attempted to reproduce the iridescence and finely pitted surface of the glass.

The very accurate similarity of this favrile agate glass *above* to the natural stone is achieved by blowing layer upon layer of multicoloured opaque glass, and then carving through the layered glass at an angle to create the effect of the striations of natural agate. The olive-green, ochre, moss green and pale yellow coloration of this example, made around 1904, is typical of Tiffany's agate vases.

This paperweight vase *above* is so called because the design is painstakingly embedded and manipulated within layers of clear glass, a process loosely akin to that found in paperweights. Design definition can vary from clear and sharp to softer and more abstract. Today, good paperweight glass with clear definition is amongst the most collectable and expensive of Tiffany's wares.

Marks
All pieces are marked, usually with the initials "LCT", in small letters. Some larger pieces bear the name in full, with perhaps a reference number. Some examples retain the original paper labels attached at the studios. The vase below is also inscribed "LCT T1690".

irregular iridescent ground. Lava glass resembles stone, and is produced by mixing volcanic slag with glass metal, a process first developed in late-18thC France. Lava glass is the most sought-after Tiffany glass today, and fetches several times the amount raised by comparable pieces in favrile or agate glass.

The flower form of this vase *above*, with its flaring ruffled rim above a band of green striated petals, is typical of the organic and naturalistic inspiration of Art Nouveau. The iridescent interior of this example is gold; others are gunmetal blue.

The glass vase *above* is unusual in being one block of solid colour – a deep Chinese red. The form is traditional, although some similar examples have necks banded in a contrasting colour with feathered decoration. This example is rare and consequently desirable.

Fakes and copies
Fakes and copies are common and collectors should develop an eye for Tiffany's distinctive style, control and use of iridescence. Faked signatures tend to be inept and, as Tiffany wares are well-documented, sequence numbers can be checked.

A contemporary, Victor Durand (1870-1931), made some excellent replicas of Tiffany iridescent art glass in conjunction with the Quezal Art Glass Company (see pp.70-1), although the shapes are generally less inventive. These were not intended to deceive and are usually marked with the name "Quezal". They are valuable and collectable in their own right.

Tiffany's lava glass, such as the vase *above*, took iridescence to new heights. Form and decoration are usually irregular, often with a dripping effect against an

QUEZAL

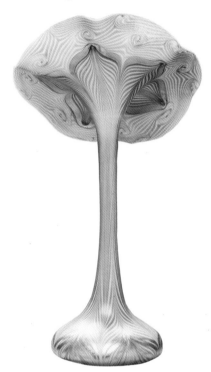

A Quezal Jack-in-the-Pulpit vase in green and gold iridescence c.1910; ht 15¼in/38.5cm; value code C

Identification checklist for Quezal art glass
1. Is the finish exclusively of iridescence, with an even, satiny surface?
2. Are the colours vibrant and contrasted?
3. Is the form asymmetric or organic?
4. Does the decoration make extensive use of the pulled feather device (see below)?
5. Is the glass more heavily walled than comparable examples by Tiffany (see pp.66-9)?

Quezal Art Glass & Decorating Co. (American, 1901-25)
Quezal was established in Brooklyn by two former employees of the nearby Tiffany Studios (see pp.66-9), using glass recipes and decorating techniques developed exclusively by Louis Comfort Tiffany. The company did little more than interpret Tiffany's popular

Favrile ware. Colours are generally striking and forms either asymmetrically or organically inspired. Most of Quezal's wares were decorative, with small vases being most common, either of ovoid or floral form, typically with bright gold iridescence on the interior, or florally inspired. The most collectable today are those modelled, like that in the main picture, as Jack-in-the-Pulpit flowers, identified by a bulbous base, an extremely slender stem, and open, spreading neck similar in form to a lily bloom. The best Quezal Jack-in-the-Pulpit vases are made to standards of artist-craftsmanship which rival those of Tiffany Studios, and can command comparable prices.

Decoration
Most Quezal glass is internally decorated, usually with striated colours forming a pulled feather type design, evident on the vase in the main picture. The better examples are also decorated on the rear of the bloom. Iridescence is usually the focus of decoration. Some simpler designs were painted just with gold lustre; these include vases of trumpet or egg shape designed to be mounted in metal stands.

The vase *above* is highlighted with crackled gold iridescence. Some rarer examples have solely blue decoration. Quezal also made some desirable lampshades in gold or blue iridescence, or in gold, white and green.

Identification
Quezal glass tends to be more heavily walled than Tiffany glass. This is evident on the ruffled rim of flower-form vases: Quezal vases and other American art glasswares generally have smooth, rounded rims.

Most Quezal pieces made after 1902 are engraved with the firm's name in large script. Some wares are also stamped with a quetzal, the exotic Central American bird-god of vivid plumage from which the company derived its name. Signed wares are collected on their own merit and Quezal signatures are sometimes faked on modern or inferior glass. Some unsigned examples were later given spurious Tiffany marks.

Other American Art Nouveau glass manufacturers
Victor Durand (1870-1931) produced art glass at the Vineland Glass Manufacturing Co. in New Jersey from 1897 until his death. Typical examples are vases of Neoclassical form in gold or blue iridescence. Durand employed Quezal artists, and many of his products resemble Quezal glass in technique and coloration. Some examples are applied with thin strands of iridescent glass in a random web. Durand wares are generally less collectable than Quezal wares.

The Union Glass Co. of Sommerville, Massachusetts, made iridescent art glass in the Tiffany style from c.1893-1920s.

The vases produced by the Union Glass Co. are often ovoid or of floral form with gold iridescence on the interior and an exterior of opaque white ground with mint green and iridescent feathering, as on the vase *above*. This combination was first used by Tiffany, subsequently by Quezal and then copied by the Union Glass Co. Most Union glass reflects Quezal's coloration, scale and standard of manufacture, but is rarer and can command high prices. Signed examples are engraved with the trademark "KEW BLAS", which the Union works used for its Art Nouveau lines.

STEUBEN GLASSWORKS

*A Steuben plum jade vase with acid-cut decoration
c.1910; ht 9in/24cm; value code B*

Identification checklist for Steuben's Art Nouveau glass
1. Is the style of the piece conventional, perhaps inspired by Neo-classical or Chinese designs?
2. Does it have more in common with English than French taste?
3. Does decoration display technical ability and precision?
4. Is the inside of the body applied with iridescence?
5. Is the iridescence even and of deep blue or gold?
6. Is the piece marked?

**The Steuben Glassworks
(American, 1903-present)**
The Steuben Glassworks was founded in 1903 in Corning, in New York State's Steuben County, by members of the local glassmaking Hawkes family and Frederick Carder. Unlike some competitors, such as Tiffany, who adhered to the artist-craftsman principle, Steuben pursued a policy of mass-production of ornamental and useful wares. Steuben ware is thus distinct from all studio glass in that the forms were intended to appeal to conventional rather than avant garde taste.

Steuben's art glass
Steuben produced over 20 distinct glass types, the best known of which is "Aurene" ware (see *opposite*). Among the many other types are "Calcite", made from 1915, a plated (cased) glass used for decorative wares and lampshades, with an Aurene finish on an opaque, opalescent ground simulating ivory; "Cluthra", a heavily bubbled and mottled glass comparable to the Scottish "Clutha" (see pp.62-3) and "Verre de Soie" – a pale, iridescent glass commonly used for stemware in the Venetian style. Among the more technically complex, rarer and more valuable wares are those with acid-cut decoration comparable in style and standard of manufacture to Peking glass. The plum-coloured vase in the main picture is a good example.

"Cintra" glass, featuring a bubbled body with interior decoration, is also particularly collectable, as is the internally decorated clear ware called "Intarsia".

example. Canes of coloured glass were arranged in bundles so that the cross-section created a pattern. Slices of *millefiori* canes could be used either as decoration, or fused together to form hollow wares. Steuben's *millefiori* wares are now among the rarest and most valuable of their commercially produced art glass.

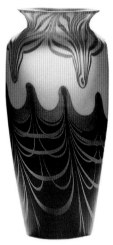

Aurene wares, produced between 1904 and 1933, account for the majority of Steuben's large output. Vases, such as the example *above*, are the most common item, but dishes and table lamps were also produced in this style. Scent bottles, which tend to be of slender baluster form, are particularly collectable, as are floriform vases, especially those decorated in the Tiffany manner with trailing leaves or pulled feather motifs. Decorated Aurene is considerably more valuable than plain. Most wares have blue or gold iridescent decoration similar to the finish popularized by Tiffany's Favrile glass (see p.66), but always with a smooth, even surface. The vase *above* combines both blue and gold iridescent decoration.

Frederick Carder (British, 1864-1963)
Frederick Carder established his reputation at Stevens & Williams (see pp.64-5) between 1881 and 1902. He served as Art Director at Steuben for over 30 years.

Among the most innovative glass types he introduced was *millefiori* ("thousand flower") glass, of which the bowl *above* is an

Carder also produced some Aurene wares; the vase *above* was decorated by him.

Marks
Aurene Ware is usually acid-stamped on the base with a fleur-de-lys and the word "Steuben" on a scroll. The more complex glasswares, such as *millefiori* pieces, bear the signature of the craftsman and are thus especially appealing to collectors. Some of those signed by Carder are also dated.

Recent production
During the 1930s, Steuben produced some strikingly elegant Art Deco glass designed by Sidney Waugh and Walter Dorwin Teague. Otherwise, since Carder's departure from Steuben in 1934, the company has produced clear, cut and engraved crystal of high standard, and continues to prosper on a site adjacent to the Corning Musuem of Glass. Wares made after 1932 are marked with "Steuben" or just "S", engraved.

THE HANDEL COMPANY

*A reverse-painted glass and bronze Handel table lamp
c.1920; ht 23in/58.5cm; value code A*

Identification checklist for Handel lamps
**1. Is the base made of bronze, or of white metal with a
patina simulating bronze?**
2. Is it weighted?
3. Is the shade painted on the interior?
**4. Does the exterior surface of the shade have a texture
simulating "chipped ice"?**
**5. Is the neck of the shade fitted with a bronzed metal
collar?**
6. Is the piece signed?
7. Do any metal fittings also have an impressed signature?

**The Handel Company
(American, 1885-1936)**
The Handel Company was
established by Philip Handel
(1867-1914) in Meriden,
Connecticut, home to several
lamp manufacturers. The success
of the company was largely due
to the rapid spread of domestic
electricity in the United States.
Before 1900, Handel decorated
bought-in glass blanks used for

kerosene lighting. However, by
the early years of the 20thC they
were designing, making and
decorating all types of lamps,
including ambitious shade
designs in leaded glass of Tiffany
type (see pp.66-7) mounted on
metal bases.
   The company's most
commercially successful products
were their reverse-painted table
lamps (see *opposite*).

Reverse-painted lamps

"Reverse-painting" refers to the American method of hand-painting the interior of glass lampshades with floral patterns or landscapes. Handel produced reverse-painted table, boudoir, floor and hanging lamps. The shades are either domed (such as the example in the main picture), conical or hemispherical, and finished on the exterior with a frosted crackle called "chipped glass" which diffuses the light. This base is bronze, although most were made of white metal with a patina simulating bronze.

Marks and fakes

Most Handel lamps bear a painted signature, a design number and perhaps the artist's name or initials on the shade rim interior. Metal bases have "Handel" either moulded or on a stitched tag fixed to the felt base. Fake shades exist: most are vertically ribbed and betrayed by poor standards of artistry.

Value is largely determined by decoration. Autumnal landscapes or allover floral decoration, as on the example *above*, are common and raise only moderate prices. Venetian or tropical island scenes are more unusual, especially those decorated and signed by Henry Bedige: the shade *below*, painted by Bedige, could fetch twice as much as the floral shade.

Handel also made exterior-painted and leaded glass shades, and a range of art glass, called "Handel Ware". Enamel-decorated, chipped glass was called "Teroma". The vase *above* is an example. All the pieces in this range were inferior to contemporary European products but are avidly collected in the United States.

The Pairpoint Corporation (American, 1880-1958)

The Pairpoint Corporation of New Bedford, Massachusetts also made lamps in the Handel manner, together with a range of innovative reverse-painted, moulded table and boudoir lamps called "puffy" lamps, with uneven glass shades. Bases vary: some simulate bronze, some are designed to resemble tree trunks, or are ribbed, others are made from gilt metal. Figural designs are very collectable.

* Other American manufacturers include Duffner and Kimberly, and the Miller and Jefferson Companies.

CERAMICS

A Leuconde porcelain vase designed by Georges de Feure, c.1900

Along with glass, ceramics offered perhaps the most malleable medium for the expression of Art Nouveau ideals, both from a sculptural and a utilitarian point of view. Forms would never again be as novel as during the Victorian era, yet innovative manufacturing and decorative methods, combined with attempts to unite form and function, revolutionized ceramic design. Led by the French and the Americans, potters employed all manner of earthenware, stoneware and porcelain in their expression of the contemporary style.

The most dramatic innovations came in the development of new glazes, some of which reflected the design preoccupations of the period. In the United States, Grueby (see pp.106-7) developed a series of glazes that imitated the texture of leaves and succulents. In Hungary, Zsolnay (see pp.92-3) produced some startling iridescent glazes similar in character to those pioneered in England by William De Morgan. French iridescent wares were largely restricted to those produced by Clement Massier (see p.93), who pioneered the development of iridescent glazes; other French ceramists appear to have preferred working with clean white porcelain typified by the wares decorated by Georges de Feure and retailed by Siegfried Bing, such as the vase *left*. Some iridescent pottery is hard to tell from iridescent glass; however, the base of a piece of glass tends to have a smoothed-out pontil mark, while the outer rim of pottery may be ground to reveal the granular texture.

Forms tend to be organic or symbolic, with decoration transferred, hand-painted or slip-trailed – a method which enjoyed a revival at this time. In France, members of the École de Paris, including de Feure, produced wares decorated with stylized plant or figurative motifs. Draped maidens were also popular; the Bohemian firm Royal Dux (see pp.86-7) produced a range of ornate shell bowls festooned with diaphanous-clad nymphs. These found an eager public, especially in Europe and the United States; it is hard to know whether it was the novel form or erotic elements which stimulated the enthusiasm.

Britain's contribution to Art Nouveau ceramics includes Minton's secessionist wares (see pp.100-1) and Macintyre's Florian ware designed by William Moorcroft (see pp.98-9). The firm of Pilkington used some Art Nouveau-inspired forms with experimental glazes. Bernard Moore's flambé-decorated wares often bear naturalistic motifs inspired by Art Nouveau, including animals and birds, fish, owls and bats. Royal Doulton's most successful attempts at an Art Nouveau style are their few exhibition wares (see pp.102-3).

The Scandinavian interpretation of Art Nouveau tended to centre on palettes of pale blue, grey and pink. The Swedish firm, Rörstrand (see pp.96-7), produced some pieces with relief floral motifs painted in soft colours.

In complete contrast to those attempting to unite form and function, the work of some firms was novel at the expense of practicality – for example, Rozenburg's teawares (see pp.88-9) were meant more for cabinet display than use. New methods meant that other artwork of the period, such as lithographs, could be captured in glaze and used to adorn a variety of vessels. A few domestic ceramic wares received the Art Nouveau treatment – for example, toilet pedestals of traditional form were printed with Art Nouveau designs.

The Art Nouveau style found some expression with studio potters. Max Läuger (see pp.80-1) applied hand-made pots with slip-trailed, stylized grasses and flowerheads. Also in Germany, Villeroy and Boch produced stoneware art pottery mechanically incised and colour enamelled, occasionally in a Mucha-type style as part of their extensive range of Mettlach ware.

Condition is crucial in valuing ceramics of this period. However, it is preferable to have a cracked piece by a top designer than a less important piece in mint condition. Unfortunately, although pieces by top designers and artist-decorators are likely to be marked, the majority of mass-produced wares from the period are unsigned.

SÈVRES

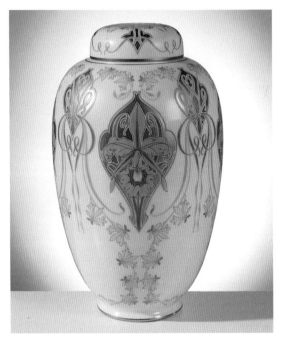

*A Sèvres vase decorated by Henri-Joseph Lasserre
c.1912; ht 9in/22.5cm; value code C*

Identification checklist for Sèvres porcelain
1. Are form and decoration harmonized?
2. Is the palette relatively subdued, including soft greens, mauves and yellows?
3. Is the piece signed?
4. Is it slip-cast?
5. Has the decoration been hand-painted in underglaze colours?
6. Is it predominantly floral?
7. Is the porcelain pure white?
8. Is the piece of unusual, sculptural form, perhaps Chinese-inspired?
9. Is it highlighted with gilding?
10. Does it have a gilt bronze base or plinth?

Sèvres (French, 1750-present)
Sèvres was founded under royal patronage at Vincennes. From 1756 the firm operated from the Hauts-de-Seine factory at Sèvres. The 19thC wares kept the forms popular during the 18thC, with decoration making play of their celebrated reserve colours, such as *bleu céleste* and *rose pompadour*. Around 1900 Sèvres began to produce Art Nouveau pieces, now acknowledged as among the finest of the period, and Sèvres vases had a huge impact on the 1900 Paris Exhibition.

Decoration

Sèvres' Art Nouveau wares were slip-cast and purely decorative. The vase in the main picture, known as *vase d'Ormesson*, echoes a popular Chinese form. Motifs, usually floral, were hand-painted in underglaze against a pure white ground. The palette of soft mauve, pink, green and yellow, evident on this vase, is similar to that used at Royal Copenhagen (see pp.94-5). The fine gilding is typical of Sèvres' high-quality wares. Plinths were essentially extensions of the ormolu mounts popular during the 18th and 19thC, and were often integral to the piece.

Bronze mounts appear on several Sèvres designs of this time – this one was made by Edgar-William Brandt.

Taxile Doat (French, born 1851)

Doat, a porcelain decorator and designer, worked at Sèvres between 1875 and 1905 and advocated a more avant-garde approach to design.

Some Doat vases take unusual shapes of organic inspiration; the bottle *above* is designed as a gourd with the gourd flower as the stopper. Doat's work has a strong Neo-classical element; he avoided the common Art Nouveau wispy maidens.

Pâte-sur-pâte decoration

Doat often used the *pâte-sur-pâte* technique of decoration, whereby a cameo-like motif is built up in layers of white slip. The medallions on the gourd are white *pâte-sur-pâte* on green.

Marks

From 1900, Sèvres used a triangular mark containing "Sèvres" or "S", with the year, (*below, left & centre*), impressed or relief moulded.

Individual decorators sometimes added their own mark. Taxile Doat incised his entwined initials (*above, right*). Decoration by a known, reputable artist may make a piece more collectable, but is not vital in assessing value.

The shapes from the Art Nouveau period tend to be more sculptural than previously. The innovative form of the *vase de Chévilly*, *above*, is known as *à pans*, meaning that the vase is rectangular or square when seen in cross section.

Collecting Sèvres

It is only in recent years that Sèvres' Art Nouveau porcelain has become keenly sought after and it is still underrated compared to some Art Nouveau ceramics. Hence this is a good investment area.

MAX LÄUGER

An earthenware vase designed by Max Läuger
c.1900; ht approx. 8in/20cm; value code F

Identification checklist for the art pottery of Max Läuger
1. Is the decoration trailed in slip?
2. Do decorative motifs include long-stemmed flowers and wispy grasses?
3. Is the piece marked?
4. Is the piece stoneware?
5. Is it robust in appearance?
6. Is the ground of one colour?
7. Is the glaze slightly irregular?

Max Läuger (German, 1864-1952)
Max Läuger, an architect, engineer and sculptor, began experimenting with ceramics at the end of the 19thC. He was one of the very few potters working in Germany to be influenced by the activities of his French contemporaries, and the decoration of his pieces almost invariably takes French-style floral or organic forms. His work is robust, with strongly innovative elements.

Läuger attempted to integrate form and decoration; this is clearly demonstrated by the earthenware double gourd vase in the main picture. The applied handles continue to the bottom of the vase, giving it an organic feel.

Läuger's distinctive decorative style involves naturalistic motifs, usually long, slender-stemmed flowers and grasses, painted in trailed slip on a stoneware body, often of slender, tapering form, coated with a one-colour reserve.

The pottery vase *above* is typical of Läuger's wares. The painted decoration, consisting of stylized, honesty-type circular decoration hanging from trailing stems, gives the piece a naturalistic appearance. The cobalt blue glaze is slightly irregular, a common characteristic of Läuger's ceramics.
* As well as vases, Läuger designed decorative tiles in an Art Nouveau style, as well as some ceramic sculpture.

Marks
Läuger's ceramic designs were produced at the Tonwerke Kandern in Baden, where Läuger was artistic director from 1895 to 1913. Most wares bear the Kandern mark (*below, left*), and Läuger's monogram (*below, right*).

ALBIN MULLER (German, 1871-1941)
The work of Albin Muller, a fellow German architect and designer, is in stark contrast to that of Läuger. In Germany in the late 17thC there was a vogue for grey stoneware with a blue glaze. Although sometimes referred to as *gres des Flanders*, most of these wares were in fact produced by potters in the Westerwald region of Germany. During the late 19thC and early 20thC, several designers in the region, including Muller, were inspired to produce similar wares with a peculiar Teutonic emphasis, a style referred to as Jugenstil, meaning "youthful-style" – the German equivalent of the term "Art Nouveau".

The stoneware pitcher *above* is typical of Muller's Jugenstil wares: the frieze decoration involves stylized flower, beaded or pod forms, historically popular in the Westerwald region. The piece has a hinged pewter cover in the 18thC manner – the German metalwork industry worked in tandem with the pottery industry.
* Muller also produced pewter wares for Eduard Hueck, a German metalworking firm.

Glazes
Most pieces are salt glazed, although some have a high, lead-based glaze.

Attribution and value
Muller is one of the few known artists of the region. However, some interesting pots were made by artists about whom little is known; this lack of information keeps prices low. Research may reveal more about obscure artists, and the area could open up.

Marks
Muller's ceramic wares may bear a printed mark similar to that *below*. They were manufactured by the Burgau porcelain factory and by Ernst Wahliss.

MICHAEL POWOLNY

*A porcelain figure of a boy with flowers by Michael Powolny
c.1910; ht 16in/40.5cm; value code C/D*

**Identification checklist for the figural ceramics of Michael
Powolny**
1. Is the piece of white earthenware?
2. Is any detailing picked out in black?
3. Is the figure an elegant young woman or a small boy,
perhaps holding a bouquet of flowers or sitting on a snail?
4. Are any stylized floral motifs incorporated into the
figure?
5. Does the subject have a cherubic aspect?
6. Is the base restrained, with a chevron-type design?
7. Is the piece distinctly Teutonic in appearance?

**Michael Powolny (Austrian,
1871-1954)**
Powolny, a ceramics decorator,
co-founded a factory, Wiener

Keramik, in 1905, together with
Bertold Löffler. Among others,
the firm also employed some of
the Wiener Werkstätte designers

(see pp.22-3 and 60-1). Powolny worked mainly in earthenware, which he preferred to porcelain. He produced several distinctive series of solid, figural, purely decorative pieces, the most notable being his line of small, cherubic boys, some of which are shown grasping bouquets of stylized flowers, as in the main picture. Other examples in the series show the boy sitting upon an enormous snail. Invariably of white earthenware, these figures are detailed in black. Despite the Teutonic appearance of the child, the flowers signify a sympathy with French figures in their similarity to the decorative details on some French furniture designs. The base of the piece is typical in its restraint and chevron-type design.

Powolny produced some bas relief wares, of which the figure of the woman *above*, is an example. Again, the subject is cherubic in appearance, and flowers are integral to the design. The figure has a distinctly Neo-classical feel; other examples exhibit a more modern, geometric influence. Powolny's bas relief wares employ the coloured majolica-type glazes favoured by Weiner Werkstätte designers, such as Josef Hoffmann and Dagobert Pèche.
* Powolny's wares are rare and not usually signed, although the characteristic style should be proof enough of their having been designed by him.

GOLDSCHEIDER (Austrian, 1885-1953)

Goldscheider, another Viennese firm, was founded for the manufacture of porcelain, faïence and terracotta. Far more prolific and commercial than Powolny, Goldscheider mass-produced a whole range of figures more in the mainstream of accepted Art Nouveau. Some figures were classically-inspired; others were of a more genre type, depicting goose girls; several featured sea nymphs, a traditional Art Nouveau motif.

Goldscheider also designed figures as electrical fittings for table and hall lamps. The terracotta lamp *above*, entitled *Chère*, is typical. The three light bulbs are located in the cloak held above the woman's head. Goldscheider tended to use surface enamels that emulated bronze patination; this can be clearly seen on the lamp.

Other wares

The firm produced novelty objects, such as fish tanks decorated with pottery figures, as well as masks which, along with their popular figures, remained in production into the Art Deco period.

MEISSEN

A Meissen vase and cover by Julius Konrad Hertschel 1905; ht 9in/23cm; value code D

Identification checklist for Meissen studio wares produced before 1910
1. Is the design symmetrical?
2. Is the form relatively simple?
3. Is the piece marked?
4. Is there a shape number?
5. Is decoration predominantly floral?
6. Is the glaze matt or semi-matt?
7. Is the ground toned?

Meissen (German, c.1710-present)
Founded at Meissen, near Dresden, this firm was the first to produce true porcelain as developed by the Chinese. The soft paste porcelain produced by Sèvres during the mid-18thC provided the first real competition: otherwise, Meissen has kept its reputation as Europe's premier producer of tablewares and figures. During the 19thC, the firm rested on its 18thC laurels, adapting their traditional forms to suit modern

tastes, with the emphasis on technique and decoration rather than novel shapes.

Meissen's Art Nouveau wares used earlier forms and applied them with contemporary designs in under-glaze decoration and matt or semi-matt glazes similar to those used on Rookwood wares of the same period (see pp.104-5), or with crystalline glazes inspired by the works of Royal Copenhagen (see pp.94-5) at the Paris Exhibition of 1900. The majority are purely ornamental.

By 1910, some Meissen designs began to show the influence of the Vienna Secessionists (see pp.172-3); the vase and cover *below*, made c.1912, borrows a Secessionist form and palette. As on earlier Meissen wares, the porcelain itself is the main feature, rather than simply providing a canvas for the decoration.

Decoration
In the early 20thC, Meissen used mainly raised *pâte-sur-pâte* decoration and trailing flowers: the vase in the main picture features a clematis. Despite its organic nature, the design is symmetrical – Meissen's Art Nouveau designs tend to be more symmetrical than other European ceramics.

Other designers
Meissen awarded some commissions to successful designers; amongst the most reputable were Henri van de Velde (see pp.18-9), Richard Riemerschmid and Paul Scheurich. Otherwise, despite their reputation, Meissen produced few great names during the period and little is known of most of their artists and designers.

Marks
Meissen wares bear the factory's blue painted crossed swords, *below, left*. On wares produced between 1860 and 1924 the swords may include a curved guard. Pieces made in 1910, the firm's jubilee year, bear the dates "1710, 1910". Some may have an artist's mark – for example, the work of van de Velde may bear his monogram, *below, right*.

ROSENTHAL (German, 1879-present)
Rosenthal wares are simple and restrained in both form and embellishment. The firm produced some fine-quality tableware decorated using a blue and white palette similar to Japanese Makuzu wares (see p.19). Some vases have *pâte-sur-pâte* decoration. Motifs include landscapes and exotic birds.

Rosenthal is best known for its figural groups, many of which featured fawns and nymphs in underglaze pale blue, grey, brown and skin tones, similar to those of the single figure shown *left*. Other popular figural subjects include mythological characters, and occasionally, small boys.

BOHEMIAN CERAMICS

An earthenware Amphora portrait vase made by R.S.K.
c.1900; ht 9in/24.25cm; value code E

Identification checklist for the "Amphora" porcelain wares of Riessner, Stellmacher and Kessel
1. Does the piece feature a mystical, regal woman?
2. Is the figure shown face on, probably against a woodland setting?
3. Is her head set against a gilded, halo-type surround?
4. Is the form exotic?
5. Is the piece highlighted with gilding?
6. Are any handles of branch or whiplash form, possibly terminating in a number of tendrils?
7. Is any decoration of moulded leaf, berry or stem form?
8. Is the piece a vase?

Riessner, Stellmacher and Kessel (R.S.K) (Austrian, established 1892)
This porcelain manufactory, established at Turn-Teplitz in Bohemia (now Austria), is best known for its "Amphora" porcelain which appeared early in the 20thC.

Amphora wares
The Amphora range consisted of mass-produced vases decorated with incise-moulded outlines upon thick onglaze enamels, a method popular during both the Art Nouveau and Art Deco periods. The more exciting examples bear portraits of

mystical, regal women, usually with a gilded, halo-like surround to the head. Most subjects are, like the woman in the main picture, shown in a woodland setting. The vessels were often of exotic form, perhaps with moulded decoration in the form of leaves, berries and stems, and with branch or whiplash handles.

Other wares

Although Amphora vases were the highpoint of R.S.K's wares in terms of design, their other productions followed similar Art Nouveau themes. A series of wall-hung masks depict other figures, such as wood nymphs. These are fairly small (about 9in/22.8cm in diameter) and relatively rare. They tend to be marked "Amphora", which suggests that R.S.K. attempted to capitalize on the success of their premier vase range by adopting the term generally.

R.S.K. produced a number of pieces with ivory glazes decorated with matt greens and sometimes dusted with gilt. A series of extremely ornamental dishes were produced in this style, with all-over decoration.

Marks

Vases are marked with the word "Amphora" and "RSK", sometimes accompanied by a mark containing three stars within a burst of sunrays (see *below*). The vase in the main picture is printed on the underside with the starburst mark and the extended legend, "Turn Teplitz Bohemia R. St K. Made in Austria" accompanied by an impressed trademark "Amphora".

Ernst Wahliss (Austrian, 1863-1930)

As a ceramics retailer, Wahliss acted as agents for the likes of R.S.K. and Zsolnay. Around 1880, he established the Alexandria porcelain works at Turn-Teplitz, home of R.S.K. It was under that firm's influence that he began to produce figural moulded vases, although his examples tend to be more

sculptural and with less emphasis on decoration. His figures often have an ivory glaze washed with sepia tones.

Duxer Porzellanmanufaktur, or Royal Dux (Austrian, 1860-mid 20thC)

Royal Dux was the most prolific of the three Bohemian firms. They followed a safe path with a range of wares depicting classically-inspired maidens holding various items, dogs and German Goths. A few examples are a little more risqué.

The colouring and fussy style of this bust *above* is typical of Royal Dux porcelain. The facial details are carefully picked out. Other wares include shell vases and bowls in an Art Nouveau style and Arab figures on camels, elephants and dogs.

Marks

The firm's mark is a salmon pink triangular pad mark impressed with "Royal Dux" in arch form. "Bohemia" appears on wares made before 1918. In 1918 the firm moved to Czechoslovakia; pieces made after this date will bear the word "Czech". Some wares carry both marks and were probably made c.1918 or held, undecorated, in stock.

ROZENBURG

*A Rozenburg eggshell pitcher and pair of vases
c.1910; ht 11in/29cm; value code C*

Identification checklist for Rozenburg's eggshell wares
1. Is the piece surprisingly lightweight?
2. Is the form elegant and inventive?
3. Is the piece marked?
4. Is it finely hand-painted?
5. Does it incorporate slender-stemmed flora and/or colourful exotic birds?
6. Does the design show an Arab influence (see *opposite*)?
7. Is the piece slip-cast (see p.177)?
8. Is the base slightly concave?

Rozenburg (Dutch, 1883-1916)
The Rozenburg pottery concentrated initially on simple earthenware. However, in the late 1880s and 1890s the firm led a revival of Dutch ceramics, and its eggshell earthenware is now considered to be among the finest earthenware ever produced (see *right*). During this period, decoration became more obviously influenced by both Art Nouveau and Japanese art. Leading designers included Theodorus A. C. Colenbrander, Sam Schellink and J. Juriaan Kok, artistic director from 1895.

Eggshell earthenware
Under Kok's directorship, Rozenburg won fame for its "eggshell porcelain", a range of extremely thin, delicate earthenware of pale ivory colour. The range, introduced in 1889, included vases, ewers and tea wares, usually in exotic shapes. Designs were often elongated, a characteristic evident in the "iris" pitcher in the centre of the main picture. The square base is also typical: the factory's eggshell wares were often designed in square section, a feature more easily visible on the pair of

"chrysanthemum" vases flanking the pitcher. All three pieces were decorated by Sam Schellink who, together with W. P. Hartgring, was among Rozenburg's finest decorators. It can be difficult to tell their work apart (see **Marks**), although both are collectable.

The Rozenburg palette is typically vibrant, and decoration is always in complete harmony with the form. Wild flowers, either elongated or swirling, are often featured.

Rozenburg wares often have elongated loop handles which emanate from rims or lips or, as in this eggshell teapot, *above*, evolve from the shoulders or sides, to give an organic feel.
* Bases are slightly concave apart from a rim of approximately 1½in (0.6cm).
* Because Rozenburg wares are slip-cast, the joints are not visible.
* Being hand-painted, no two pieces are exactly alike.
* Birds were popular subjects, especially on wares decorated by Hartgring and Schellink.

Condition
Rozenburg wares were designed to be purely decorative rather than useful. As a result of their vulnerability, most were displayed as cabinet pieces. The wares are now extremely expensive, due to their high quality and great beauty, and the condition of pieces is thus extremely important. Because the raw material was somewhat elastic, any cracks can cause the piece to warp or pull away on either side of the crack.
* Some pieces exhibit very fine crazing over the whole body.
* No fakes or copies are known.

Early wares
Some of the firm's earlier "Arab" wares emulated Iznik and Persian earthenware in both form and decoration. The pottery also produced landscape tiles. Most are decorated with standard Dutch landscapes with figures in interior settings.

Rozenburg's earliest wares tend to be decorated using the darker, more subdued palette evident on this earthenware plaque, *above*. Motifs were fairly stylized, and used forms of a relatively traditional type. Decoration was often all over.
* In 1906, the company introduced their range of "Inkrustierte Fayence". These wares are sparsely decorated with colour enamels enclosed within deep incise-moulded outlines. "Juliana Fayence", introduced in 1910, used busy decoration in a colourful palette on a cream earthenware body.

Marks
Rozenburg wares typically bear one of the following two marks:
* "ROZENBURG DEN HAAG", printed with a stork, *below*; after 1900, this was surmounted by a crown device

* a painted monogram and year symbol. Decorators had their own monogram.

OTHER DUTCH FACTORIES

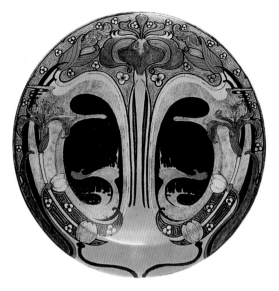

*A Brantjes earthenware dish with painted decoration
c.1900; dia 17½in/44.5cm; value code D/E*

Identification checklist for Brantjes ceramics
1. Are the motifs predominantly floral?
2. Is strong use made of symmetrical decoration?
**3. Is the decoration all over, possibly with a dark blue
reserve, and outlined in black?**
4. Is the form symmetrical?
5. Is the piece earthenware?
6. Are the glazes bright?
7. Is the piece signed?

Dutch ceramics
During the Art Nouveau period
Dutch ceramics followed two
distinct courses. The first of
these was the traditional blue and
white wares for which the town
of Delft had become world
famous from the middle of the
17thC. The second type was the
art pottery which developed
during the 1880s and which in
turn can be divided into two
distinct schools: the Hague,
where there was a preference for
floral decoration making great use
of sinuous curves and both
symmetrical and asymmetrical
decoration, probably best
exemplifed by the wares
produced at the Rozenburg

factory (see p.88-9); and the
Amsterdam School, which
concentrated on simpler forms
and formalized, sometimes
geometric decoration, probably
best exemplified by the wares
produced at the Amstelhoek
Factory.

Weduwe N.S.A. Brantjes & Co.
(Dutch, 1895-1904)
This shortlived factory, although
based in Purmerend, had some
affinities with the Hague School. It
concentrated on decorative
earthenwares, usually with strong
forms and bright, floral
decoration like that on the dish
in the main picture. Some of the
designs may have been

inspired by the pattern books of the French potter, Maurice Pillard Veneuil. The firm merged with the Haga factory of the Hague (established 1903), and its name changed to N. V. Haga. The name was changed again in 1905, to Plateel Bakkerij.

Brantjes was not afraid of experimenting with novel forms, as this two-handled vase *above* shows. As with the plate, decoration is all over and very brightly coloured.

Amstelhoek (Dutch, 1894-1910)
This factory was founded by the goldsmith W. Hoeker as a ceramics workshop for the sculptors Lambertus Zijl and Christian Johannes van de Hoef,

who produced earthenwares decorated with inlaid designs in coloured clays on ochre or brick red grounds. In 1896 a metalware department was opened.

Amstelhoek's main ceramics designer was van de Hoef, who designed the Egyptianesque *jardinière, above*. Typically, this is slip cast but has a hand-crafted appearance. In 1903/4 van de Hoef moved to Haga (see *above*).

Other factories
* Zuid Holland, 1898-1964. This Gouda-based factory is best known for its use of relatively dark, sombre palettes and stylized floral and fruit decoration with semi-matt glazes. The firm also produced some wares inspired by the early 20thC Rozenburg pottery produced under Colenbrander.
* Arnhem Fayencefabrik, 1907-1928. This firm concentrated on symmetrical stylized flower-and-leaf decoration.
* Ram Factory, 1920-28. This shortlived factory was founded by Colenbrander in Arnhem.

Distel (Dutch, estab'd 1895)
Distel's main designer between 1895 and 1896 was Bert Nienhuis, a well-known painter and designer. The arrival of Theodorus A.C. Colenbrander led to a more colourful

interpretation of floral and other designs. Colenbrander advocated the use of bold abstract designs with large areas of reserve, repeating some of the shapes he had used while at the Rozenburg factory (see p.88-9).

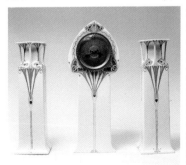

Nienhuis used mainly white glazes with restrained decoration often applied in soft pastel colours. As in this clock set, *left*, designs were symmetrical. Nienhuis moved to Hagen in Germany in 1912, but returned to Holland in 1917 and worked as a studio potter making mostly undecorated work using a variety of glaze techniques.

ZSOLNAY

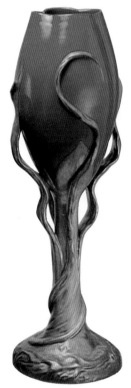

A monumental Zsolnay tulip-form lustre vase 1900; ht 28in/72.5cm; value code C

Identification checklist for the ceramics of Zsolnay
1. Does the piece have a multi-coloured iridescent glaze, or several contrasting iridescent glazes?
2. Does it depict naturalistic foliage or female figures?
3. Is any decoration moulded in low relief?
4. Is the form simple, or, if ornate, is it naturalistically-inspired?
5. Is the piece signed?
6. Is it thickly potted?

Zsolnay (Hungarian, established 1862)
This ceramics firm made the greatest Hungarian contribution to the development of the Art Nouveau style in eastern Europe. Established at Pécs, Funf-kirchen, the firm produced ornate, Islamic-inspired pierced wares until the 1890s. Following the appointment of Vincse Wartha as artistic director in 1893, Zsolnay began to produce decorative wares using organic forms and iridescent glazes inspired by French ceramics, particularly those of Clement Massier (see *opposite*).

Typical features

Zsolnay's Art Nouveau vases were often relatively simple in form. They were sometimes decorated with low relief-moulded detail. Motifs often included tree silhouettes and dark ruby skies, with a lustrous surface. Other wares, like the tulip-shaped vase in the main picture, relied more upon pod-like naturalistic forms, with moulded leaves and branches picked out in contrasting iridescent colours. The iridescent glaze used for the tulip head was known as Eosin. It was developed in 1894 by Vilmos Zsolnay and Vinsce Wartha, and made popular by the factory from the turn of the century until well into the 1920s.

* Some monumental pieces are more than 3ft (1m) in both height and diameter.

The lustre vase *above* has low relief-moulded decoration of maidens dancing under a starlit sky. Moulded decoration was usually applied to simple forms such as this; the decoration of more ornate pieces was integral to the form.

Marks

All Zsolnay pieces are marked. The earliest mark is a pad mark with an integral medallion impress-moulded, showing the five towers of Pécs, where the firm was based. Later marks were variations on the early design. Printed marks were also used, often in underglaze blue.

This exuberant, iridescent, fish-shaped vase *above* bears the Zsolnay factory seal on its underside. The form is among the most inventive produced by the firm.

CLEMENT MASSIER
(French, 1845-1917)

Massier took over his father's pottery workshop in 1883. He produced earthenware vases and plaques with subtle iridescent or lustre decoration, as well as a range of miniature vases. Forms were primarily a canvas for decoration.

The plate *above* was designed and decorated by Lucien Levy Dhurmer, one of Massier's leading designers . Typically, the decoration is applied over an opaque underlying glaze.

* Factory signatures are either painted or impress-marked; artists' signatures or initials are painted.

The Rock and the Wave, *a porcelain group by Theodor Lundberg 1899; ht 18in/46cm; value code D/E*

Identification checklist for Royal Copenhagen ceramics
1. Is the colouring pale, the palette consisting predominantly of blue-grey and flesh tones?
2. Does the piece display a real sense of movement?
3. Is it marked?
4. Is the form inventive?
5. Is the piece of high quality?
6. If the figure is a child, is it demure and in a pastoral setting?
7. Is it slip-cast and hollow inside?

Royal Copenhagen (Danish, 1775-present)
This firm was established and run under royal auspices until 1883. Arnold Krog, a ceramic artist, became art director in 1883 and introduced innovative glazing and decorative techniques which revolutionized output during the Art Nouveau years.

Wares
The piece in the main picture
was designed by Professor
Theodor Lundberg in 1899, and
is a classic Danish porcelain
figure. Slip-cast, and hollow
inside, it would have been mass-
produced and hand-painted. The
symbolism, composition and
overall sense of movement are
strongly Art Nouveau, as are the
woman's flowing tresses.

Marks
The Rock and the Wave is still
produced today, and it can be
difficult to differentiate between
old and modern examples.
However, marks have changed
over the years, and can offer a
clue to dating.

The mark *above, left* was used
from 1894 to 1900, the *centre* mark
between 1894 and 1922, and the
mark, *right*, from 1905. The firm's
Parian wares are marked
"ENERET", meaning
"copyright".

Glazes and decoration
In 1886 Krog introduced a
decorative technique whereby
wares were painted in
underglaze, and then applied
with a crystalline glaze with the
surface appearance of snowflakes
or crystals, developed by
Valdemar Engelhardt.

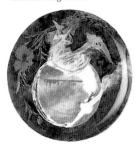

The dish *above* has been hand-
painted by Krog and applied with
Engelhardt's distinctive crystalline glaze. The seascape is
typical of the naturalistic
decoration favoured by Krog.
The artist has treated the dish as
a canvas, leaving areas in the

white, and the resultant blue and
white effect shows a distinct
Japanese influence. However,
Royal Copenhagen's crystalline-
glazed wares are more commonly
decorated in a soft palette of blue
and grey.

Other wares
In 1908 the firm produced the
first in a series of year plates,
painted in soft blues, with a
different design for each year.
Early plates are highly
collectable. The series is still in
production today. Also made
were realistic bird figures,
tablewares in novel, naturalistic
forms, including teapots with
dragonfly-shaped handles, and
commemorative plates.

BING & GRONDAHL PORCELLAENSFABRIK
(Danish, 1853-present)
This Copenhagen firm produced
Art Nouveau-inspired pieces in
stoneware and earthenware.
Their best-known designer, F.
August Hallin, had worked at
Royal Copenhagen.

The tulip form and floral
decoration of the Bing &
Grondahl vase *above* echoes
Krog's preoccupation with
naturalism. The evident
Japanese influence is typical of its
designer, Effie Hegermann-
Lindencrone, as is the pierced
decoration. The piercing has left
the vase unusable and therefore
exclusively decorative.
* In 1888 the firm introduced the
revolutionary and internationally
acclaimed "Heron" service,
named after the near all-over
decoration of painted herons.

RÖRSTRAND

A Rörstrand tea service
c.1900; value code C (the set)

Identification checklist for Rörstrand porcelain
1. Does the piece incorporate relief moulded decoration?
2. Does the palette consist of blue, grey and pink on white all-over reserves?
3. Is the piece colour-enamelled under the glaze?
4. Is it marked?
5. Is the form relatively simple and balanced?
6. Is the piece relatively thickly potted?

Rörstrand (Swedish, estab'd 1726)
This pottery, near Stockholm, was the premier Swedish porcelain factory at the turn of the century. The firm produced faïence, initially in the English style, and later revived earlier European styles. Their interest in European forms led them to absorb the popular French Art Nouveau into their repertoire.

Rörstrand wares have simple and balanced forms, often incorporating relief moulded decoration and colour-enamelling with a subdued palette of blue, grey and pink against overall white reserves, displayed by all the pieces shown here. The porcelain itself is of a good colour and is often fairly thickly potted. The firm also produced a range of wares decorated with crystalline glazes applied to simple elegant shapes, as well as some wares that compare with contemporary

designs produced by Sèvres (see pp.78-9), in form and decoration.

Wares tend to combine usefulness and decoration; simple vases and ashtrays are often moulded on the rims with butterflies or other insects. The handles and saucers of the tea set in the main picture are shaped like dragonflies, a motif typical of Art Nouveau. The whole set contains 28 pieces; single items of unusual form are comparatively more collectable.

Rörstrand porcelain is available in large quantities in the United States; the British appear to have preferred the more conservative porcelains of Copenhagen (see pp.94-5). Rörstrand's inventive forms and attractive palette found favour with Siegfried Bing (see pp.16-7), who is known to have sold several examples to the Victoria and Albert Museum in Kensington, London.

The simple, pure white vase *above* typifies Rörstrand's staple wares from c.1900. The relief-moulded poppy design is typically restrained. The poppy motif was popular with Art Nouveau designers.

Rörstand produced a quantity of Japanese-inspired ceramics which compare favourably with the work of the contemporary Japanese art potter, Makuzu. The example *above* shows a definite Japanese influence both in form and the restrained decoration. The leaf decoration is typical of many of Rörstrand's Art Nouveau pieces.

Designers
Alf Wallander designed for the firm from 1895 and became art director in 1897. He introduced Art Nouveau to the firm, by modelling relief floral decoration painted with soft underglaze colours. The architect Ferdinand Boberg and his wife Anna also designed for Rörstrand, as well as the rival firm of Gustavsberg.

Marks
The firm's 19thC wares were printed with the word "RÖRSTRAND", or simply the letter "R". From 1884 a printed mark was used incorporating the three crowns of Marieberg.

Rörstrand

Arabia (Finnish, 1874-present)
This Helsinki-based porcelain factory, founded as a subsidiary of Rörstrand, became independent in 1916. The firm mass-produced vases, often with leaf or geometric motifs in an Art Nouveau style.

The chief designer from 1895 was Thure Oberg, who decorated vases and lamps with complex Art Nouveau designs. In 1902 the company introduced their "Fennia" series of wares, designed by the celebrated architect Eliel Saarinen.

The form of the vase *above* is of Dutch inspiration. The unusually bold design suggests this is probably an early piece; the subdued design of the tea service in the main picture is more typical.

WILLIAM MOORCROFT

A Macintyre Florian ware "Iris" vase, designed by Moorcroft c.1900; ht 10in/27.5cm; value code D/E

Identification checklist for Moorcroft's "Florian" wares
1. Is the design typically florid or does it make use of naturalistic motifs?
2 Is the decoration tube-lined (see p.101 and *opposite*)?
3. Is the piece earthenware?
4. Is it hand-made?
5. Is it marked?
6. Does the decoration complement the form?
7. Is the piece decorated all over?
8. Is it symmetrical or does it include a symmetrical element?
9. Has use been made of burnished gilt reserves?

William Moorcroft (English, 1872-1945)
From 1898, Moorcroft headed the Art Pottery department of Macintyre & Co, the Staffordshire pottery firm established c.1847 at Burslem. His early designs, known as "Aurelian" wares, were generally printed in underglaze blue with overglaze iron-red and gilt and decorated with designs reminiscent of the textiles of William Morris. His later work for Macintyre, retailed as "Florian ware", was possibly the foremost British contribution to Art Nouveau ceramics.

Florian wares

At Macintyre, Moorcroft produced designs for both utilitarian wares and the now more collectable art pottery, including vases, jugs, loving cups, biscuit barrels, dessert wares and jardinières. His inventive forms, applied with original designs, echoed the fabric designs, not only of William Morris, but also those popularized by Liberty. Moorcroft's Florian designs were often symmetrical, and depicted various flora, usually applied to slender vases or ewers, and irises, like those that decorate the vase in the main picture.

This rare "butterfly" vase, *above*, is a departure from Moorcroft's traditional style. The asymmetrical design is unusual, as are the yellow butterflies around the slender neck. Moorcroft rarely used animals or insects in his designs, although he produced a fish design during the 1920s and 30s. However, the use of tube-line decoration applied over an ivory ground is typical.

The three-handled tyg (or loving cup) *above* is typical of Moorcroft wares in that it features "tube-line" decoration, a hand-applied network of fine lines of slip (a mixture of clay and water) applied to the surface. Decoration on Florian wares tends to cover the whole surface of a piece. Interiors are usually glazed and interior decoration may creep over the rim of a piece. Wares with a cream or near-ivory body have more sparse decoration. Ivory-bodied wares also make use of gilding; this tyg has gilded areas around the rim, and gilded details on the handles.

Signature and marks

Moorcroft signed all Florian wares, usually "W. MOORCROFT des", and sometimes with "JAMES MACINTYRE & CO FLORIAN WARE" printed in brown in a cartouche, or just "WM des".
* Pieces marked "MOORCROFT BURSLEM" are post-1913. Patterns commissioned by Liberty include the printed mark "made for Liberty & Co."

Peacock feathers, like those that adorn this Florian ware vase, *above*, c.1900-2, were a favourite Moorcroft motif. This piece is a good example of Moorcroft's well-balanced designs and careful integration of form and decoration: the peacock feathers are better suited to the fuller shape of this vase than would be the slender irises that adorn the slender, tapering vase in the main picture.

MINTONS, LTD

*A Mintons, Ltd jug in the Viennese "secessionist" style
1904; ht approx. 14in/35.5cm; value code F*

Identification checklist for Mintons "secessionist" wares

1. Is the decoration tube-lined (see *opposite*)?
2. Is the glaze runny or uneven?
3. Is the piece signed?
4. Is the form avant-garde or unusual?
5. Does it consist of stylized flora?
6. Is the piece earthenware?
7. Is the palette predominantly purple, ochre and white; tomato or blood-red; or leaf green or turquoise?
8. Is the decoration all-over?

Mintons, Ltd (1793-present)
This pottery was established at Staffordshire in 1793, since when it has remained at the forefront of the production of innovative art pottery, with a wide range of wares exhibiting a high level of craftsmanship. Under Leon Solon, director 1900-09, Mintons produced a range of earthenware influenced by the work of the Secessionists, the association of avant-garde artists, architects and designers whose work epitomized the Viennese Art Nouveau style, with their flowing plant shapes and geometrical patterns. Many of Mintons' "secessionist" wares

are decorated using tube-lining, a method whereby lines of slip are piped on to a piece like icing (confectioner's sugar) and fired. Glazes are then painted in between the piped lines. Raised lines of slip can be clearly seen in the tube-lined jug shown in the main picture.

The glazes of Mintons' tube-lined wares tend to be uneven and often overrun the confines of their raised slip boundaries. The red decoration on the vase *above* has run beyond its boundary and up towards the neck of the piece. Well-defined decoration places examples at a slight premium, as the less controlled pieces can sometimes appear a little unsightly.

Palette

Minton's ''secessionist'' wares feature a striking palette – purple is common, often used to dramatic effect with ochre and white, as can be seen on the jug in the main picture. Tomato or blood-red was also popular, usually set against leaf green or turquoise, as on the vase. The colour combinations, many of which had never been used on English pottery before this date, tend to be vibrant, almost shocking.

* Although it was thought that Leon Solon and Philip Wadsworth designed in collaboration for Mintons, it is now recognized that Wadsworth designed the more staid, sober pieces, whilst Solon's work is more exuberant.
* Mintons' range included jardinières (often on pedestal bases), vases, ewers and candlesticks.
* The decoration tends to be carefully united with a complementary form.

FOLEY (English, 1892-1925)

Foley became the trade name for another Staffordshire pottery, Wileman & Co, which was known as Shelley from 1925. The company continued to produce ceramics under the name Foley, after their premises, The Foley at Longton. Foley Art Nouveau wares included a range of earthenware designed and decorated by the English-born ceramist, Frederick Hurten Rhead (1880-1942), using a dramatic form of underglaze decoration known as *intarsio*, which involves colour enamelling on transferred outlines, set against a dark terracotta body.

The jardinière *above*, by Rhead, has animal and figural decoration. Floral and Persian motifs were also common. Other wares include vases, umbrella stands, and a selection of novelty teapots depicting political personalities of the time, such as Paul Kruger and Joseph Chamberlain.

Although a number of wares were produced under the Foley name at this time, including some advertising wares, *Intarsio* is the most important range of the period. Pieces generally have ''Foley Intarsio ware'', printed in black on the underside.

Production tailed off after Rhead emigrated to the United States in 1902, to work for the Roseville pottery.

DOULTON & CO.

A "rabbit" vase decorated by Mark V. Marshall for Doulton 1910; ht 20in/51cm; value code B

Identification checklist for Doulton ceramics
1. Does any decoration consist of stylized flora?
2. Is the form relatively simple, with complementary decoration?
3. Does the piece bear the artist's or modeller's incised initials?
4. Does the palette include traditional tones of ochre, green and cobalt blue?
5. Does the glaze have a streaked effect?
6. Is there a factory mark on the underside of the base?

Doulton & Co. (English, 1815-present)
Between 1826 and 1956, Doulton & Co. occupied premises in Lambeth, London, producing commercial and industrial stoneware and porcelain figures. In 1883, a second factory opened at Burslem, Staffordshire which concentrated on the manufacture of earthenware and bone china, notably earthenware dinner services and bone china tea sets. The firm became Royal Doulton in 1901, under warrant from Edward VII.

Doulton's designers

One checklist cannot convey the variety of wares produced by Doulton during the Art Nouveau period: the company employed many designers, each with their own distinctive style. A long association between Doulton & Co. and the nearby Lambeth College of Art provided the firm with many innovative ideas.

Mark Villiers Marshall, designer of the rabbit vase in the main picture, was one of their most prominent designers. He was best known for his grotesque animal subjects in salt-glazed stoneware with low relief and rich ornament, similar to those produced in Britain by the Martin Brothers. Rabbits were an uncommon Art Nouveau motif, and the tube-line method of decoration, used on this piece, underwent a revival during this period. Marshall also modelled salamanders, frogs and lizards, and some more graceful figures.

Other designers

Marshall captured the spirit of Art Nouveau, but it was the stoneware decorated by Frank Butler, a deaf and dumb artist, that really pre-empted the Art Nouveau style. Active at Doulton between 1872-1911, Butler's carved and modelled designs bearing relief patterns set against grounds decorated with circles, dots or lines, were generally better executed than Marshall's.

Other Doulton designers of this period include Arthur Barlow, sisters Florence and Hannah Barlow and John Eyre.

The tile panel *above*, entitled *Sleeping Beauty – The Fairies at the Christening*, was painted by Margaret Thompson, an illustrator who specialized in tiles and vases. She painted mainly sylph-like fairy figures with delicate wings, often in the striking purple, green and white palette seen here, with their features and anatomies outlined in black.

* Several children's hospitals in England commissioned murals from Doulton; St Thomas's Hospital in London has recently restored some panels painted by Margaret Thompson and William Rowe.

The shape of the tureen, *above*, echoes the French Empire style, and the floral design and the palette resemble pieces produced by French factories such as Sèvres. However, the style is Art Nouveau. The decoration was applied using the Lactolian technique, whereby slip is painted on bone china, then overglazed.

Marks

All wares are marked, either "Doulton Lambeth England" or "Doulton Burslem England", impressed, printed or painted.

ROOKWOOD

A Standard glaze vase decorated by Matthew Daly for Rookwood
c.1886; ht 44½in/113cm; value code B

Identification checklist for Rookwood Standard wares
1. Is the piece earthenware?
2. Is the decoration painted in coloured slips under a clear, high glaze?
3. Is the piece marked with an impressed signature, date, code letters and an incised artist's signature?
4. Do decorative motifs include American flora, fauna, landscapes or portraits of American Indians?
5. Is the piece heavily potted and slip cast (see p.177)?
6. Does ground colour blend from one tone to another?
7. If a vase, is the form of Japanese inspiration?

Rookwood (American, 1880-1960)

Maria Longworth Nichols founded this Cincinatti pottery to produce wares that combined Japanese ideals of craftsmanship and aesthetics with naturalistic imagery. By 1900 Rookwood was the most important American Art Pottery, with a good European reputation gained at the Paris Exposition of 1900, and it is not uncommon to find Rookwood wares in Europe.

Decoration

Decorative motifs used at Rookwood include indigenous American flora, fauna and landscapes, and often show the influence of the Nancy School (see pp.12-5), particularly in the depiction of flora. The vase in the main picture is decorated with sunflowers, a recurrent Art Nouveau motif.

Wares bearing portraits of American Indians, particularly those decorated between 1897 and 1903 by Matthew Daly (the artist of the vase in the main picture), and William McDonald, are particularly sought after.

"Standard" glazes

Standard glaze wares, first made in 1883, tended to be heavily potted, slip cast and painted in coloured slips under a clear, high glaze. The ground often tones from one shade to another – that of the vase in the main picture shades from a rich amber to umber. Other Standard colours include "Sea green", a pale green ground, "Iris", a pale, muted grey, and the mottled "Goldstone" or "Tiger-eye".

In 1904, Rookwood patented a matt glaze called "Vellum". Vellum-glazed wares tend to bear stylized flora or forest landscapes similar to some contemporary French overlay glass. Many vases have wisteria decoration, as does the example, *above*, from c.1910.

Fakes and copies

Rookwood has not been faked, but several potteries, such as the Roseville Co., produced wares similar to Standard glaze wares. Many are marked, but unmarked examples are distinguished by signs of inferior manufacture, such as visible seams and crudely executed decoration.

Marks

Most wares are impressed "ROOKWOOD" and dated, with perhaps an artist's monogram. From 1886, "RP" was used (see *below, left*). A flame device was added, one flame for each year from 1887 to 1900 (see *below, centre*). From 1900 the last two digits of the year were impressed in roman numerals below the monogram (see *below, right*).

THE GRUEBY FAIENCE CO.

A melon-shaped vase designed by Ruth Erickson for Grueby c.1900; ht 11½in/28.5cm; value code C

Identification checklist for Grueby art pottery
1. Is the piece thickly potted in porous, buff earthenware?
2. If a vessel, is it slip-cast?
3. Is the form simple and possibly Japanese-inspired?
4. Is the glaze thickly applied and with a pitted texture?
5. Is the piece monochrome with a matt finish, probably rich green?
6. Does any relief ornament have a tube-lined outline?
7. Does any decoration feature prominent foliage?
8. Is ornament minimal and of vertical emphasis?

The Grueby Faience Co. (American, 1894-1930)
William Grueby (1867-1925) trained at the Low Art Tile Works in Boston, Massachusetts, which produced tin-glazed earthenware, architectural faience and press-moulded, glazed tiling in the English taste. After he founded his own firm in East Boston, he continued to use processes learned at Low Art, such as the application of thick opaque glazes. He produced mainly architectural faience, tiles and sanitary wares, many of which were designed to reflect and complement the Arts and Crafts furniture and furnishings popular at the time.

"Watermelon" glazes
Grueby won international acclaim at the Paris Exposition of 1900 for their thickly potted vases, with matt, monochrome glazes thickly applied to give a textured and pitted effect similar to that of cucumber or watermelon skin. This effect was compounded by the firm's favourite glaze, a rich, organic, moss green. Some wares take forms that could be described as "melon"; the example in the main picture was designed by Ruth Erickson, one of the most collectable of Grueby's artists.
* Grueby's melon-shaped vases are the most desirable of their wares.

Shapes are organic and stylized: the vase *above* is in the formalized shape of a lotus flower. The mustard yellow of this glaze was used for vase bodies as well, as was ochre, deep blue, pink and greyish purple. Pieces decorated in more than one colour are particularly popular.

Shapes and motifs often combine to create an organic effect; the bulbous shape and stylized leaf and flower decoration of the vase *above* reflect the naturalistic preoccupation of Arts and Crafts. Broad leaf motifs, including lotus, acanthus and tulip, are often used to create vertical ribbing, used on the lower section of this vase. Vertical emphasis has been created with the stems of stylized flowers.
* Grueby made a few lamp bases in the same bulbous shape, with unflared necks suitable for fitting with oil fonts.

Collectability
Impressively large examples of Grueby wares are most collectable, particularly those with blossom decoration, usually highlighted in yellow and white. Pieces made before 1910 are also particularly sought after.

Tiles
Grueby tiles tend to be thickly slab moulded in porous, pale buff earthenware; the most desirable are glazed in a muted palette with a matt finish. Decoration is usually stylized and is often tube-lined – that is, outlined in thin trails of slip.

Some tiles were designed as part of a landscape series. The seven tiles shown *above* are part of a set of 14 depicting a landscape of sky and palm trees. Naturalistic designs such as this are very collectable, as are medieval designs, some of which are reminiscent of the work of the British ceramist William de Morgan. Other common motifs include turtles, illustrations from Lewis Carroll's nonsense poetry and prose or images from the works of Rudyard Kipling. A few examples are deeply relief moulded.
* Grueby tiles are generally unsigned, although some tile backs do bear an impressed company name and lotus blossom trademark (see *below*).

Marks
Fully marked wares, bearing the firm's name, sometimes in a roundel with a lotus leaf trademark *below*, and an artist's monogram, are very collectable.

Particularly desirable artists' marks are those of Ruth Erickson, George P. Kendrick and Wilhemina Post.

GEORGE E. OHR

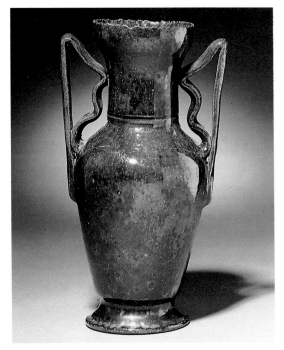

*An earthenware vase with applied handles by George E. Ohr
c.1895; ht 9in/23cm; value code C*

Identification checklist for Ohr's art pottery
1. Is the vessel of unusual, even bizarre, form?
2. Does it have the appearance of amateur studio pottery?
3. Are the walls, handles or rim crimped or folded in an apparently random manner?
4. Is the vessel thinly potted, making it lightweight and brittle in appearance?
5. Is the glaze mottled and lustrous and of deep colour?

George E. Ohr (American, 1857-1918)
George E. Ohr was a great eccentric and a virtuoso art potter, although never a commercial success. He opened a rather rough and ready studio in the artist's colony of Biloxi, Mississippi in 1885, and worked alone but for a brief association with Newcomb College Pottery (see *opposite*) in the mid-1890s. His eccentric lifestyle and appearance (he looked like

Salvador Dali) earned him the nickname "the mad potter of Biloxi". Most Ohr ware now available to collectors comes from his sizeable personal collection (over 6,000 pieces) made as a legacy for his children and on the market since their recovery from storage in 1972.

His work is unique. Using a wheel and a wood-burning kiln, he produced hand-thrown pieces with the appearance of amateur-made, studio pottery. He worked almost exclusively in red earthenware and pieces tend to be thinly-walled with the lightweight and brittle, eggshell-like appearance evident on the rim of the earthenware vase in the main picture. Some pieces have applied ornament, such as the handles on this vase; these examples are likely to raise higher prices, partly because they tend to be larger and more complex in design.

Ohr made both useful and ornamental wares including vases, mugs, teapots, jugs and inkwells. His work is particularly popular with American collectors and museums.

Ohr's favourite modelling technique was to pinch and fold vessels into unusual, even bizarre shapes prior to firing. The extreme irregularity of the vase *above*, particularly of its rim, is characteristic of Ohr's work.

Glazes
Ohr's glazes are usually lustrous, mottled and of the green or brown colours easily achieved in his wood-burning kiln, like the brown spotted glaze on the vase in the main picture. More rarely, he used bronze or rich black glazes, or perhaps more striking glazes such as the unusual salmon and orange glaze on the vase above.

Marks and copies
Most of George Ohr's pottery is signed, usually impressed "G E OHR Biloxi Miss"; later examples bear an incised facsimile script signature. Ohr's ceramics are easy to copy, and their popularity has led to a number of forgeries which bear convincing marks and can be difficult to distinguish from the originals. Copies are commonly small-scale with a very red body and a mirror-black lustrous glaze.

NEWCOMB COLLEGE POTTERY (American, c.1895-1945)

Founded at Newcomb College, New Orleans, this pottery was active until the end of World War I, and produced some of the rarest, most valuable American art pottery. Operated mainly by women, it developed a distinctive style of thrown wares decorated with incised patterns of local flora highlighted in polychrome slip. Examples from before 1910 typically have a high glaze, whilst later wares tend to have a semi-matt finish. The range included small, ovoid or globular vases, drinking mugs and tea ware.

* All Newcomb pottery is hand-made and decorated and fully signed with "NEWCOMB COLLEGE" or an "NC" monogram incised or impressed, a body letter (Q or W) and an artist's monogram or cipher. The larger wares are the more collectable, as are those featuring landscape decoration or those known to be by the better artists, such as Mary Sheerer or the founder, Joseph Meyer.

Newcomb Pottery's most characteristic palette combined blue with green, yellow or white. This typical coloration is evident on the high-glazed vase *above*, decorated with stylized irises, produced at the pottery c.1905 by Sabina Elliot Wells.

TECO

A Teco vase designed by William J. Dodd
c.1910; ht 11in/29cm; value code A/B

Identification checklist for Teco pottery
1. Is the body stoneware?
2. Is it heavily walled?
3. Is the piece slip-cast, with crisp outlines ?
4. Does the design have an architectural feel?
5. Does it incorporate protruding or undercut elements, suggesting complex moulding techniques?
6. Is the glaze thickly and evenly applied?
7. Is the glaze metallic and monochrome?

Teco (American, 1902-c.1923)
William Day Gates established Gates Potteries at Terra Cotta, Illinois, in 1881, for the manufacture of architectural terracotta, tiles and bricks. He introduced "Teco" stonewares in 1902 (the name was derived from the first and third syllables of the town name). Unlike other American pottery of the period, Teco wares were mass-produced in large industrial kilns using sophisticated slip-casting and glazing methods. The wares, which include garden ornaments, pots and vases designed by local architects, have an architectural

feel and tend to be heavily walled, with good, crisp outlining. Some display complex moulding, with protruding structural elements; the 12 reticulated leaves on the vase in the main picture are intrinsic to the moulding. The designer of the piece, William J. Dodd, favoured reticulated patterning. The organic form was also common.

* Modern collectors are particularly interested in those examples that reflect the "Prairie" style advocated by Frank Lloyd Wright (see pp.36-7).

The vase *above*, designed by Gates himself, has the metallic, evenly textured, pale green, matt glaze resembling oxidized copper typical of Teco ware. Other glaze colours include deep blue, plum, yellow and brown. Gates executed a number of designs, mainly in the architectonic style. The protruding buttresses of this vessel are again evidence of complex moulding techniques.

Availability
By 1911, the Teco range of stoneware numbered over 500 designs. Small, plain examples are relatively common, but impressive pieces by the firm's more sought-after designers, such as Fritz Albert (whose work tends to feature local flora symmetrically arranged), William Dodd and William Day Gates, are rare and highly collectable, particularly in the United States.

Marks
Pieces bear an impressed or stamped design number, usually of 3 digits, with one of two possible marks (see *below*), in vertical print. Artists did not sign their wares but can often be identified by the style.

ARTUS VAN BRIGGLE (American, 1869-1904)
Van Briggle began his career at Rookwood (see pp.104-5). He opened a studio in Colorado Springs in 1901, to produce fine interpretations of French Art Nouveau, such as vases with floral or figural relief decoration.

The vase *above*, entitled *Lorelei*, is moulded as a female figure whose arms, head and hair form the rim. Pieces have matt glazes – this bluish-green was the most common colour, and others include deep and pale blue, plum, brown and off-white. The most collectable wares, produced before Van Briggle's death in 1904, bear an incised date. Later, undated examples, are common and of little collectable value.

111

SCULPTURE

La Nature, *a gilt and patinated bronze bust by Alphonse Mucha, 1900*

The popularization of small scale sculpture and statuettes during the Victorian period meant that sculpture became available to a wider audience in the early 20thC. More than any other popular media of the Art Nouveau period, sculpture managed to cross the boundary separating applied and decorative arts. The work of French sculptors such as Raoul-François Larche (see pp.116-7), Agathon Léonard (see pp.116-7) and Louis Chalon (see pp.114-5) took the spirit of the movement to probably its most dramatic peak. Form and decoration became increasingly interdependent and sculptural elements began to be used to decorate useful objects such as figural table lamps. Raoul-François Larche and Leo Laporte-Blairsy (see pp.118-9) were the first sculptors to apply their sculptural forms to the then novel invention of electric light, and Larche's table lamp sculpted in the image of Loïe Fuller, an American dancer, was among the most successful of all Art Nouveau lighting devices (along with Tiffany's jewel-like table lamps, see pp.66-9).

The female form predominated as the central decorative element, usually endowed with an ethereal, dreamlike expression accentuated by flowing tresses of hair. Naturally-inspired forms and motifs were also important.

While their Continental counterparts advocated a strong symbolistic approach, British sculptors concentrated more on impressionistic elements. The English treatment of the bronze relied more on the ethics of the New Sculpture, a movement that had emerged during the 1870s, led by the likes of Frederick, Lord Leighton and Sir Alfred Gilbert, which aimed to break the shackles of the Neo-classical past through a more naturalistic representation and less static, more impressionistic stances. In certain instances a strong link with romanticized medievalism is retained. Even so, female figures often adopt similar serene or mysterious expressions and hair tends to be *en chignon*.

Of the various casting methods used during the period, sand-casting, whereby a piece was cast in sections, then joined and patinated, was the most common. Bronzes cast using the *cire perdue* (or "lost wax") method (see p.176) command a premium, although value will obviously be determined by the importance and reputation of the artist. It is vital that bronzes retain their natural finish and have not been polished. The patination should have deepened and matured naturally over the years and, if damaged, will reduce value.

Most pieces are signed and many bear a stamped or incised foundry mark, perhaps confirming that the piece is *cire perdue*. However, not every signed piece is genuine. A Larche lamp with the right foundry mark may be a copy – many have been produced in Paris in the last 15 years. Faked sculpture abounds. Most is of inferior quality, with suspicious, unconvincing patination, often excessively worn in the wrong places. Forgers sometimes force dirt from vacuum cleaners into the oiled crevices in an attempt to falsify age, and fakes can be very hard to detect. Lamps should always be checked for genuine electrical fittings, but some good fakes include original fittings. Dubious examples should be shown to an established expert.

Much Art Nouveau sculpture was mass-produced in Germany, albeit with shapes and motifs based on French examples. The work of the Viennese Gustav Gurschner (see pp.126-7) is the most exciting and collectable, although it has only recently begun to be fully appreciated. Particularly important are his figural table lamps that include iridescent glass shades made by Loetz (see pp.56-7).

Very little sculpture of high style was produced in the United States during the Art Nouveau period. Prominent collectable American sculptors include Whitney Frishumth (1880-1980) and Frederick William MacMonnies (1863-1937).

MAURICE BOUVAL

A pair of Bouval gilt-bronze lamps
c.1900; ht 20in/50.5cm; value code A

Identification checklist for the sculpture of Bouval
1. Is the subject a mysterious female figure, possibly with closed or downcast eyes?
2. Is the piece made of gilt-bronze?
3. Does it bear the sculptor's signature as well as the foundry seal?
4. Does it incorporate strong naturalistic elements?
5. Does the subject appear to interact with, or become part of, nature?
6. Is the marble base of good quality?

Maurice Bouval (French, d.1920)
Along with Leo Laporte-Blairsy (see pp.118-9), Bouval was a pupil of the French realist sculptor Jean-Alexander-Joseph Falguière (1831-1900). At the 1900 Paris Exhibition, Bouval exhibited his metalwork designs, which included ormolu candleholders and silver paper knives. However, he is best known for his lamps and busts, which generally feature mysterious female figures that give the impression of merging with nature, and are often entwined or draped in leaves and foliage. In the pair of bronze lamps in the main picture, the naked figures seem to grow out of the swirling base and are entwined in the iris-shaped stems (which conceal light fittings). Both women have their eyes closed, a common feature of Bouval's subjects. Bouval's other work includes inkwells, covered boxes, pin-trays and other useful objects, usually in bronze.

Comparison with Mucha
The strong similarity between Bouval's bronzes and those of the Czech artist Alphonse Mucha (see pp.162-3), meant that for many years Bouval's work was considered a poor imitation of Mucha. However, Bouval's style is now appreciated and demand for his work has increased in the last ten years.

them than do Bouval's. They generally lack the dreamy quality of Bouval's maidens, and are more powerful. Chalon often combined media in his work; for his sculpture of *Cleo de Merode* (of which the piece *below* is another version), he combined gilt–bronze and silvered bronze.

Bouval was not prolific and, of his relatively few larger pieces, it is versions of this bust, *above*, that turn up most frequently at auction. The subject's serene downcast gaze and aura of mystic symbolism reflect the preoccupation of many Art Nouveau designers with mysterious, melancholy women. The entwined leaves and flowers are typical. This piece stands on a high-quality plinth of dark red marble – a well-cut plinth like this generally indicates a high-quality piece, as do the green onyx bases on the lamps in the main picture. Bouval's most famous bust, *Ophelia*, is similar in style and form to this example.

Marks
Bouval's work is usually signed "M. Bouval", and may bear the foundry mark, in the case of the pieces shown here, of the Parisian firm, Thiébaut Frères.

LOUIS CHALON (French, dates unknown)
The work of Louis Chalon resembles that of Bouval in a number of ways. He also produced lamps and busts, and his mantel clocks, vases and dishes usually feature a female figure emerging from a flower. However, Chalon's female studies tend to have more life to

The gilt-bronze lamp *above* anticipates the work of the Art Deco sculptors through its strong geometry and the dramatic stance and confidence of the female subject. The subject, the dancer Cleo de Merode, hailed by Chalon as the embodiment of the new optimistic spirit ushered in by the 1900 Paris Exhibition, was one of his favourite subjects.

The piece combines decorative and useful functions very well. The woman's stance and her sunburst ornament suggest illumination, and the electrical fittings seem to grow out of the outstretched branches.

Marks
Chalon used both the engraved signature and monogram, *below*, to mark his pieces. The bronze lamp is marked "CHALON", and bears the seal of the founder, E. Colin & Cie of Paris.

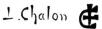

RAOUL LARCHE

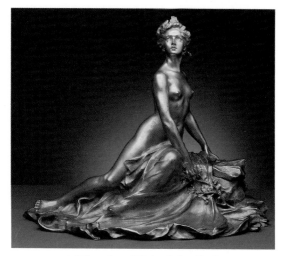

A gilt-bronze figure of Wisdom *by Raoul Larche c.1902; ht 19½in/49cm; value code A*

Identification checklist for the metalwork of Larche

1. Is the piece bronze, possibly gilded?
2. Does it convey a strong sense of movement?
3. Does it bear the marks of the designer and the foundry?
4. Does it have a secondary function?
5. Is the base integral with the figure?
6. Is the subject female?
7. Has attention been paid to meaningful facial expression?
8. Are there erotic undertones to the figure?

Raoul-François Larche (French, 1860-1912)

Larche's reputation is based mainly on his dramatic gilt-bronze female figures, in particular a famous series depicting the American actress and dancer, Loïe Fuller (see *opposite*). His work invariably involves women, whether in the form of a nymph appearing from a seashell, a dancer or a symbolic or allegorical figure such as *Diana* or *Wisdom*. He made great play of the female form, both naked and sheathed in diaphanous drapery.

Larche's work is typical of the way some Art Nouveau sculptors moved away from pure fine art towards a more functional, decorative art: the allegorical figure of *Wisdom* in the main picture conceals a hinged

inkwell. Most of his work is gilt-bronze and made using the sand-casting method, by which pieces were cast in sections, and then joined and patinated. The gilt-bronze surface should be intact. Some pieces have been erroneously polished until the bright surface underneath is revealed, which reduces value. Larche also mass-produced some figures from models by other bronze foundries or ceramists.

Marks

Larche sculptures always bear an incise-cast signature as well as the seal of the Paris founder, Siot Décauville. This may appear as "SIOT FONDEUR". The seal features as a small circular medallion on the base of the piece (though not the underside).

Loïe Fuller, the subject of the figural lamp *above*, was regarded as a living embodiment of Art Nouveau. Similarly, although the facial detail of this piece is less precise than on the figure of *Wisdom*, the strong sense of swirling movement inherent in Larche's Fuller bronzes has led to their being considered among the finest Art Nouveau bronzes ever produced. There are two known versions of this lamp.

Beware
Very good fakes of Larche's work abound. It is important to compare a piece with one that is known to be genuine. Be suspicious of a lack of wear on the base, or an excessive amount of wear on areas not normally susceptible. However, a new light fitting does not necessarily indicate a fake: many genuine pieces will have received updated fittings over the years.

AGATHON LÉONARD
(French, b. 1841)
Léonard worked for Sèvres, producing biscuit figures in the Art Nouveau style for table decoration. One series of at least six dancers, *Le Jeu de l'Echarpe*, was used as the model for the gilt-bronze statuettes for which he is best known. Léonard often combined a number of media – for example, bronze and marble.

Like the figure *above*, the dancers from the *Jeu de l'Echarpe* series are realistic, if stereotyped. They invariably wear high-waisted, pleated gowns, the wide sleeves of which almost form flowerheads. Facial detail tends to be quite severe, and hair is arranged *en chignon* (in a roll at the back of the head).

Some of Léonard's pieces, like the bronze *Femme Chauve-Souris* (Bat woman), *above*, show the high symbolism of Art Nouveau. The figure's partial nudity and zoomorphic features, such as the batwings, give it a sensual, decadent mood.
* Pieces are marked "A. LÉONARD SCLP, M" and bear the seal of the casting foundry, "SUSSE FRERES EDITEURS".

117

A silvered bronze and glass lamp designed by Leo Laporte-Blairsy c.1900; ht 16in/41.5cm; value code A

Identification checklist for Laporte-Blairsy's sculptural metalwork
1. Are form and function successfully integrated?
2. Is the subject female, or of organic inspiration?
3. Is the piece bronze?
4. Does it have a signature and the mark of the foundry?
5. Has a lot of attention been paid to detail?

Leo Laporte-Blairsy (French, 1865-1923)
Laporte-Blairsy studied sculpture and first exhibited his quality silver and jewelry designs at the 1900 Paris Exhibition. Like Larche and Léonard (see pp.116-7), he favoured flowing, sensuous lines. His designs successfully integrate form and function, and his lighting fixtures generally incorporate novel construction elements. In the example in the main picture, the globe held by the figure symbolic of light at night is engraved with

the same star-shaped motif which appears elsewhere in pierced and stamped form. The fine casting typically shows great concern for details, such as hair and facial features.
* The base is an integral part of the sculpture.

Motifs
As well as lamps, Laporte-Blairsy produced bronze sculptures, many with marine motifs.
* Non-figural floral light fittings often employ formalized and symmetrical arrangements.

Marks
The incised mark "LEO LAPORTE-BLAIRSY" appears, usually with the foundry seal "SUSSE FRERES EDITEURS PARIS".

THEODORE RIVIÈRE (French, dates unknown)
Rivière had a good understanding of the human form and his bronze figures tend to be anatomically accurate. His subjects were mainly theatrical and usually symbolic.

The group of Salammbo and Matho, entitled *Carthage, above,* is based on a scene from a play starring Sarah Bernhardt. The posture, expression and head-dress of the goddess-type figure of Salammbo are strongly

theatrical; a further sense of drama is added by the figure clinging to her waist.
* Unusually, decoration extends over the circular base.
* The sculptor's inscribed signature is prominent on the base.

ALBERT CHEURET (French, dates unknown)
Formerly undervalued, Cheuret's work has recently begun to rise in price, but relative bargains may still be found. He produced primarily functional pieces, such as light fittings, rather than pure sculpture. Decoration usually features naturalistic motifs. Cheuret was one of the few Art Nouveau designers to successfully make the transition to the Art Deco style.

Cheuret's work sometimes combined various media. This small table lamp, *above,* shaped like a cluster of tulips, is a good example. The piece features sinuous bronze stems and leaves, and novel shades made from alabaster. The use of this material was uncommon for the period. Cheuret was particularly fond of alabaster with silvered bronze.
* Alabaster is very soft, and prone to cracking. It is not easy to replace damaged pieces, so the buyer should ensure that any piece is complete.
* This lamp is one of a pair, although examples are available singly.
* This piece bears the incise-cast mark "ALBERT CHEURET".

119

A gilt-bronze-mounted ceramic vase by Charles Korschann c.1900; ht 25³/₄in/65.5cm; value code B

Identification checklist for the sculpture of Korschann
1. Is the subject a naked or partly clad nymph-type figure?
2. Is the base floral or organic? (The piece above is an exception in this respect.)
3. Is the piece signed?
4. Does it feature whiplash and/or natural motifs?
5. Has a lot of attention been paid to facial detail?
6. In decoration, has use been made of gilding?
7. Are there areas of differently coloured patination and/or enamelling?

Charles Korschann (Bohemian, b.1872)
Charles Korschann had considerable commercial success, but produced few exclusive commissions. Most of his work, which included inkwells, lamps, bronzes and vases such as the example in the main picture, contain figural elements.

Decoration

Korschann's work shows a fondness for naked, half-naked or diaphanously clad maidens. Typically, these slender figures have coiffured hair, and may be adorned with flowers. Korschann often used cold-painting or enamelling to produce variously coloured patination. The decoration of the vase in the main picture contrasts gilding with cobalt blue enamel, for a jewel-like effect.

Marks

Korschann's signature appears as "CH KORSCHANN". Pieces usually bear the mark of the Paris founder, Loucet.

EMMANUELE VILLANIS
(French, dates unknown)

Like his contemporary, Korschann, Emmanuele Villanis was a successful commercial sculptor who was also based in Paris.

He is best known for an extensive range of bronze sculptures, depicting maidens in typical Art Nouveau style. Like the example shown below, most of his figures are of head and shoulders only, although he did make a few full-length portraits. Unlike Korschann's, most of Villanis's work is purely decorative, apart from a few sculptural lamps.

Korschann often placed figures upon floral or organic-type bases, like the example *above*. Bases generally make strong use of whiplash motifs, as well as natural motifs such as cow parsley, both of which are found on the base of this gilt-bronze figure. The slender figure of the subject is typical of Korschann, as is the particularly detailed treatment of the facial features. The casting is of characteristically high quality.

Villanis concentrated on facial expressions which, like the bust of "Silvia", *above*, are usually soulful and dreamlike. Most pieces tend to be patinated in dark brown or dark green.
* Sculptures stand on relatively simple, pyramidal bases. These bear the title of the work modelled in low relief in distinctive lettering.
* Most carry a Paris foundry seal, together with the sculptor's signature.

121

REMBRANDT BUGATTI

A bronze elephant by Rembrandt Bugatti
1910; ht 22in/57cm; value code A

Identification checklist for the sculptures of Rembrandt Bugatti

1. Is the form slightly impressionistic?

2. Does the piece have a sculpted surface, rather than a smooth and finely detailed one?

3. Does it bear the artist's signature (and, possibly, the date)?

4. Does it also have the foundry seal of Hébrard?

5. Is the figure supported on a thin, free-formed base? (However, see the secretary bird *opposite*.)

Rembrandt Bugatti (Italian-born, 1885-1916)

As the son of Carlo Bugatti (see pp.24-5), and younger brother of Ettore, the automobile designer, Rembrandt Bugatti came from a truly remarkable family. Although his career spanned a mere 15 years, Bugatti created some of the finest animal sculptures ever produced. Unlike the 19thC animaliers, who produced precise, realistic sculptures of animals, Bugatti attempted to capture the personality or spirit of the animal. The modelling of his 150 bronze sculptures shows an acute understanding of natural forms. Bugatti concentrated on exotic wildlife, and created few studies of domestic animals. From 1907, he worked in Antwerp, home at that time of Europe's finest zoo. Antwerp zoo provided both inspiration and the models for his pieces. He was awarded the Legion d'Honneur in 1911.

Typical features
The elephant in the main picture illustrates many characteristic features of Bugatti's work:
* The impressionistic form conveys the character of the elephant, while the sculpted, uneven surface suggests the texture of the animal's skin.
* The figure stands on a thin base, or plinth.
* The patina, or surface colour of the bronze, is a rich, dark brown. On many other Bugatti pieces, the patina is nearly black.
* The piece is of a reasonable size.
* The artist's signature is visible on the plinth in front of the elephant's hind legs.

Cire perdue
Almost all of Bugatti's pieces were cast by the Hébrard foundry, which used the complex method known as *cire perdue* (''lost wax''). In this method, a hollow wax mould is first made of the artist's original clay model. This is then encased in plaster. When molten bronze is poured in, the wax melts and flows away and is ''lost''.

Marks
Although some of Rembrandt Bugatti's sculptures have edition numbers, they must also bear the artist's signature and show the seal of the foundry if they are to be considered genuine. However, fakes or copies are not so far known.

The long-legged secretary bird, shown *above*, with one wing touching the ground, is unusual for Bugatti in that the base is thick and rock-like, unlike the more typical thin base on the elephant in the main picture. The height of the sculpture suggests a reason: the base must support the weight of the bird, which might otherwise fall over.
* The piece is signed on the base.
* The brown-black patination is typical. Bugatti achieved this effect through the application of an ammonia solution with heat.

Bugatti's understanding of exotic wildlife is evident in his pieces, although the figures often seem posed. In the pair of leopards *above*, it is the stance rather than the detail of the modelling that evokes the animals' spirit and personality. The wooden plinth is uncommon, and may have been attached to the original thin bronze base some time after manufacture.

ENGLISH SCULPTURE

A bronze group, Orpheus and Eurydice, *by Charles Ricketts c.1906; ht 13½in/34cm; value code B*

Identification checklist for the sculpture of Ricketts
1. Is the subject impressionistic?
2. Is it figural?
3. Is it fairly muscular, conveying a sense of strength and emotion?
4. Is the surface sculpted, rather than smoothly detailed?
5. Does the subject seem to be emerging from the base?
6. Is the piece signed?

Charles de Sousy Ricketts (English, 1866-1931)
Of all British sculpture produced in the early 20thC, the work of Ricketts is perhaps the most impressionistic, and comes closest to the Art Nouveau style. Ricketts claimed to be the only man to understand Rodin, and the influence of the French sculptor is clearly evident in his work, exemplified by *Orpheus and Eurydice, above.*

Forms
Ricketts had a good understanding of the human form, and his figures convey a strong sense of emotion. In *Orpheus and Eurydice* the subjects typically appear to be emerging from the rockwork base. The sculpted surface and apparent lack of detailing on this piece – for example, in the hands, were intentional, and do not indicate a poor quality casting.

Collecting point

The group has been repatinated, but this should not lessen its value. Repatination can reduce the value of some sculptures by as much as 20 percent, but the rarity of this piece ensures that it will still command a high price.
* All Ricketts' sculptures bear the monogram "CR".

SIR ALFRED GILBERT
(English, 1854-1934)

Gilbert's sculptures represent the beginnings of the transition from the Victorian style to Art Nouveau.

Gilbert is usually regarded as the doyen of British sculptors in this period. Despite his strong denial of any association with Art Nouveau, he produced a large amount of work in this style. His sculptures typically capture a strong sense of emotion or of movement, as in this bronze figure of *Comedy, above*. His civic sculpture includes the famous Shaftesbury memorial surmounted by the statue of *Eros* at Piccadilly Circus in London.
* Gilbert also designed jewelry of abstract form in silver, steel wire and coloured glass paste.
* His work is usually signed.

ALBERT TOFT (English, 1862-1949)

Toft learned sculpture at Wedgwood and Elkington and Co, and opened his own studio in London, to produce bronze figural pieces, usually with rich brown patination. His work often shows the influence of the Australian sculptor, Bertram Mackennal (1862-1931). His female figures have more of an ethereal feel to them than the sculptures of Gilbert. Most wear their hair *en chignon*, and a number of subjects are cloaked.

As is evident in the bronze figure of *Peace* shown *above*, the arms of Toft's figures are often expressive and gesturing. In this example the figure holds a winged tribute; another edition of the figure holds a casket. Bases are simple, a fairly typical feature of the period. This example is cast with masks and foliage.
* Toft produced a number of civic sculptures, such as 1914-18 war memorials.
* Pieces bear an incise-cast signature.

GILBERT BAYES
(English, 1872-1953)

Another English sculptor whose very original style owed much to Art Nouveau was Gilbert Bayes. During the early 20thC, his work tended to combine Art Nouveau and medieval influences. He is known more for his bas-reliefs than for his sculptures. Bayes continued to work into the Art Deco period.

GUSTAV GURSCHNER

A bronze and nautilus shell lamp by Gustav Gurschner c.1900; ht 21in/53cm; value code A

Identification checklist for the sculpture of Gustav Gurschner

1. Is the style curvilinear and sinuous, perhaps incorporating elongated whiplash motifs or stalk-like elements?
2. Does the piece combine various media, such as bronze, glass and shells?
3. If a lamp, is the shade made of a nautilus shell, or iridescent glass, perhaps produced by the firm of Loetz (see pp.56-7)?
4. Is the piece signed?
5. If a bowl or a vase, does it incorporate bands of formalized decoration?

Gustav Gurschner (born Bavaria, 1873)

Until recently, Gurschner was regarded by many as a commercial artist working in a debased French style, but his work is now being taken more seriously. He was associated with the Viennese Secession (see pp.22-3), but worked in a fluid style that had more in common with French Art Nouveau. Much of his work concentrates on human forms. He is best known for sculptural lamps.

Lamp shades

Gurschner employed a variety of media in the creation of the shades of his lamps, including nautilus shells, such as the example incorporated into the lamp in the main picture.

shade on the bronze figural lamp, *below, left*. Like this example, many Gurschner lamps make strong use of figural forms. This piece also shows his characteristically sinuous style and elegant subject. Typically, the figures appear to grow out of the base.

* At the 1900 Paris Exhibition, the Viennese retailers Bakalowits & Söhne (see pp.58-9) exhibited iridescent glass lamps in metal mounts by Gurschner.

* This piece is marked "GURSCHNER DEPOSE" (meaning "registered"), while the piece in the main picture bears the mark "8.99 GURSCHNER", probably indicating the date of manufacture.

No item was considered too small or insignificant to warrant being given the Art Nouveau treatment, as this match striker *above* demonstrates. The symbolic low-relief panel decoration of naked maidens is appropriately emblematic of fire. This piece bears an incised signature.

FRANZ BERGMAN (Austrian, dates unknown)

Like Gurschner, Bergman also worked in Vienna. His sculptures concentrated on Middle Eastern figures such as Arab street vendors or carpet sellers. He produced several erotic bronzes and figural groups incorporating concealed levers which caused clothes to open or other movements to take place. Bergman popularized the technique of cold-painting, in which coloured enamels are annealed or painted onto bronze figures. Gurschner also employed this technique.

* Erotic bronzes feature the mark "NAMGREB" – Bergman's name backwards.

* Another Viennese sculptor at this time was Carl Kauba, whose most famous works were studies of North American Indians.

Gurschner often incorporated iridescent glass shades into his lamps, many of which were produced by Loetz (see pp.56-7), who were responsible for the

SILVER, JEWELRY AND METALWORK

A carved ivory pendant by Henri Vever, c.1900

The approach of the Art Nouveau jewelry designers challenged the accepted view that the setting was there to take as many precious stones as it could hold. Jewelry now took on a sculptural quality, and materials were chosen for their "fitness for purpose" rather than for any intrinsic value. The carving of jewels also underwent a renaissance. Subjects were naturalistic and, as in other media, included insects and flowers. The female form was also featured, often in very symbolic form.

The French dominated the field. In the vanguard of the new approach was René Lalique (see pp.130-1), whose artistry in carving and composition was outstanding. French styles were more fluid than the German and Viennese: the

Germans were more interested in abstract forms, whilst the Viennese preferred simple, highly stylized motifs. Secessionist and Wiener Werkstätte designers produced some very strong designs (see pp.138-9). Viennese jewelry is comparatively rare today. In England Liberty sold Cymric jewelry designed mostly by Archibald Knox (see pp.146-7). Charles Horner produced a range of jewelry in the manner of Liberty, and there was a revival in enamelwork under Alexander Fisher (see p.155).

The English were less innovative with silver and for the most part continued to produce their traditional Regency and Georgian wares, although to a limited degree they also managed to blend some Art Nouveau ideals with traditional silver. Again, probably the most interesting pieces came from Liberty's Cymric range, which had a strong Celtic influence. William Connell produced a range of Art Nouveau-inspired ornamental wares, including picture frames and caskets. Another original designer was Kate Harris, who produced some highly individual designs for Huttons (see pp.152-3).

French silverwares do not reflect Art Nouveau ideals to the same extent as other media, although Cardhillac produced some tea and coffee services of florid form. They seem to have been more interested in enamel *objets de vertu*, which were produced in quantity. Enamelling was also popular in Vienna. In Scandinavia the name of Georg Jensen became synonymous with organic-inspired silver forms (see pp.144-5). Some significant silver and metalwork was designed by Bindersboll. In Germany Art Nouveau forms and motifs became available to the masses through the pewter and silver plate wares of such firms as Kayser Sohn and W.M.F. (see pp.140-1). As well as sinuous stalks and pod motifs, and naked or semi-naked female forms, German pewter is distinguished by its use of entwined abstract symbols. The success of the German metalworkers inspired Liberty to introduce a range of inexpensive pewter wares, again largely designed by Archibald Knox. When buying Liberty pieces or Kayser Sohn, make sure that any glass liner is original, as these are almost impossible to replace without special commission. In Britain, metalwork was also produced by various guilds: Edward Spencer of the Artificer's Guild worked in copper (and silver); John Pearson produced copper and lustre pottery; the Keswick School of Industrial Art also produced fine art metalwork.

In the United States Tiffany Studios produced sheet bronze desk sets, and other small objects. Gorham made some interesting mixed metal wares (see pp.156-7). Other significant metalworkers were the Roycrofters, who specialized in copperwork, and Dirk Van Erp (see pp.158-9).

Silver is not much faked: British silver is hallmarked and the marks can be checked in a book of silver marks. American silver and most Continental silver is also marked. Being comparatively inexpensive, the metalwork is not usually faked, making it a good place to begin collecting.

RENÉ LALIQUE

*A blond horn and enamel butterfly stomacher
1900; ht 4-5in/10-12.7cm; value code A*

Identification checklist for the jewelry of René Lalique

1. Is the piece of fine quality?
2. Does it display a variety of constructional and decorative techniques?
3. Are there strongly naturalistic elements?
4. Does the piece combine precious and semi-precious materials?
5. Is it stamped?
6. Is use made of stones, or blister or baroque pearls?
7. If a pendant, is the chain innovative and integral to the design of the whole piece?
8. If in the form of an insect, do wings incorporate *plique-à-jour* decoration (see p.133)?
9. Is the piece colourful?

René Lalique (French, 1860-1945)

René Lalique was the foremost Art Nouveau jeweler and silversmith. His jewelry ranges from hat pins to the massive corsages designed for Sarah Bernhardt, one of his most important patrons, and includes chokers, bracelets, pendants, stomachers (worn over a bodice), brooches and hair combs. He executed few of his designs – most were hand-made by other craftsmen.

Until the late 19thC the primary function of jewelry was to display wealth; Lalique revolutionized the art by emphasizing the sculptural quality of jewels. Fitness for purpose was an important factor and, although Lalique made use of precious materials, he would only do so if they contributed to aesthetic quality. It was for aesthetic reasons that he combined materials of different intrinsic values. Tortoiseshell, horn or glass might be set within a frame of precious metal, or studded with precious and semi-precious stones such as pearls, opals or moonstones.

Decorative techniques
Lalique used several decorative techniques; the butterfly stomacher in the main picture, carved from one piece of blonde horn, is enamelled in various tones of brown. Other decorative methods include *pâte-sur-pâte* (see p.176), *champlevé* enamelling and *plique-à-jour* enamelling (see p.133), usually found on the wings of his insects. He also used oxidized silver and carved gemstones. Decorative techniques are often used to constructive effect: the strong colouring and definition of the larger butterfly here, set against smaller, paler butterflies, suggests a three-dimensional effect.

Lalique began experimenting with glass in 1902 and some of his later Art Nouveau jewelry incorporates moulded glass, sometimes with glaze effects. Although his best glasswork belongs primarily to the later Art Deco period, much of this echoes his work from the golden years of Art Nouveau.

Other chains may consist of bar links, possibly finely enamelled, or of beads of other types of stone, such as moonstone. Chains are usually integral to the design of the piece. This piece retains its original presentation box, which will add to its value.

Lalique's pieces are famous for their inspired composition. His designs are typically symmetrical, often with two supporting elements or motifs framing a design without being its central feature. The symmetrical enamelled peacocks in the pendant *above* provide a balanced frame for the central triangular opal; in their beaks they hold the pearl terminal of the neckchain, whilst from their tails hangs a decorative pearl drop.
* Some pieces are reticulated, adding a real sense of motion.

Signatures
Most early examples of Lalique jewelry are engraved ''R Lalique'', perhaps accompanied by ''France'' and a model number in matching script. The L was sometimes elongated (see p.180 for marks).

Fakes
A number of recent discoveries have been considered to be extremely dubious, which although of good quality, often fall short of the superb craftsmanship of known Lalique pieces.
* Not all Lalique's pieces were one-offs; some were made up a number of times.

As well as the use of opals, this pendant *above* displays several features typical of Lalique's work: the multiple form is common to his pendant designs and the neckchain is interspersed with opal beads.

GEORGES FOUQUET

*A Fouquet brooch in gold, semi-precious and precious stones
c.1900; lgth 3in/7.6cm; value code A*

Identification checklist for the jewelry of Georges Fouquet
1. Is the piece intricately and delicately constructed?
2. Are form or decoration inspired by purist Art Nouveau motifs, such as floral or dragonfly motifs?
3. Is the piece signed?
4. Is it numbered?
5. Does it combine a variety of media, perhaps a combination of stones and inexpensive materials?
6. Is the form inventive?
7. Is the design asymmetrical, yet with a sense of balance?

Georges Fouquet (French, 1862-1957)
Georges Fouquet was the son of Alphonse Fouquet, a Parisian jeweller known for his enamelled renaissance revival pieces. Georges' work was designed to be exclusive, and is often compared to that of René Lalique (see pp.130-1).

Forms
Fouquet experimented with a number of different styles, although he appears to have preferred a purist interpretation of Art Nouveau. His forms were innovative and tended to combine a variety of media, often of differing intrinsic values. For example, the brooch in the main

picture is made of gold, with pierced arabesques studded with rubies and a pendant sapphire, but the central motif of a woman's head is carved from semi-precious stone. Fouquet was fond of the pendant jewel form of this brooch.

translucent enamels. When the backing is removed, a transparent "stained glass" effect is achieved. The method was developed in Russia during the 17thC, but was adopted by French and English jewelers of the Art Nouveau for use in pendants and brooches.

Fouquet's work tends to be extremely well controlled. His designs are generally asymmetrical, but this does not detract from an overall sense of balance, apparent in all the pieces shown here. His jewelry is intricate; the exceptionally fine working of the delicate wings of the dragonfly *above* is evidence of his great control and skill.
* The dragonfly was a favourite Art Nouveau motif.

Georges Fouquet's sources of inspiration were diverse. As well as using motifs popular during the Art Nouveau period, he also experimented with more unusual forms. The ornamental haircomb, *above*, constructed from carved horn, opal, enamel and gold, is based on an Egyptian palmette-type pierced decoration, and the palm tree motifs and central fan motif give the comb an Egyptian feel.

Marks
Most of Fouquet's work is well documented, with many of his original drawings and designs in the keeping of the Musée des Arts Decoratifs in Paris. His pieces are invariably signed, usually with the letter "G" or with "Gges Fouquet" stamped (see *below*), and most also bear a reference number which relates to an existing catalogue.

The diamond and pearl pendant *above*, in the shape of a stylized wing, has been enamelled in lavender and light blue using the *plique-à-jour* method (see *opposite*). The form of the pendant, a cluster of flowers with pearl blooms, reflects the popularity of the floral motif in Art Nouveau design.

Plique-à-jour
Fouquet was fond of the *plique-à-jour*, or open braid, enamelling method, whereby a structure of metal strips laid on a metal background forms enclosed areas that are then filled with

Gges Fouquet

G. FOUQUET

The haircomb illustrated here is stamped and engraved with the number 4680. On the lid of its accompanying box, in gilt lettering designed by Alphonse Mucha, is the address "G. Fouquet, 6 Rue Royale Paris".

LUCIEN GAILLARD

A Gaillard enamel and diamond hair ornament c.1901; 5in/12.7cm; value code B

Identification checklist for the jewelry of Lucien Gaillard
1. Is the piece sculptural?
2. Does the design incorporate precious or semi-precious stones?
3. Is the form innovative?
4. Is the piece signed?
5. Does it incorporate tortoiseshell, ivory or horn?
6. Is it fitted with a gold mount or appliqué?
7. Is any foliage highly naturalistic?

Lucien Gaillard (French, b.1861)
Gaillard initially made his name as a silversmith c.1889, but was persuaded by René Lalique (see pp. 130-1) to design jewelry, and his designs owe much to Lalique. He is best known for his hair slides or combs in tortoiseshell, ivory or horn, and it is these pieces which turn up most frequently at auction. Gaillard's designs were always innovative, and often used a combination of mundane and more precious materials. The hair ornament in

the main picture features a standard tortoiseshell hair comb, with enamel and diamond decoration added almost as an appendage. In spite of the high degree of craftsmanship evident in this piece, particularly in the enamel work, the swallows are slightly stiff in comparison with the work of Lalique. However, the piece has a striking three-dimensional quality.
* Gaillard signed his work "L GAILLARD" or "LUCIEN GAILLARD".

134

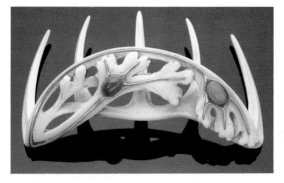

In decoration, Gaillard favoured naturalistic motifs, such as the stylized fronds set with two oval chalcedonies which make up this ivory hair comb, *above*. Unlike the piece in the main picture, the form and the decoration are integral. Sepia staining gives this comb a sense of depth.
* Many of Gaillard's pieces are accompanied by their original presentation box; such examples are often preserved in their original condition.

EUGENE FEUILLÂTRE
(French, 1870-1916)

After leaving Lalique's workshop in 1899, Eugene Feuillâtre set up his own business. His speciality was enamel work, and especially *plique-à-jour* (see pp.132-3). He continued the tradition of enamelling established at Limoges in France during the 12thC.
* Feuillâtre produced mainly *objets de vertu* – often of quite substantial size – but also produced some jewelry similar to that of Lalique, using glass, gold and silver. He perfected a technique of applying enamel to platinum jewelry.

* Feuillâtre was perhaps the greatest exponent of the *plique-à-jour* method of decorative enamelling. Probably his nearest rival in quality was Carl Fabergé, the Russian jeweler and silversmith. One of the most famous examples of the art, a large silver dish decorated with grotesque fish in polychrome enamels, is made to Feuillâtre's design.

The quality of casting on this mounted and enamelled giltbronze vase, *above*, is characteristically high. The use of enamelling against a toned silver background is unusual, as is the perspective of the piece. Again, the form involves a combination of symmetrical and asymmetrical elements.
* Most pieces bear an engraved signature, "FEUILLÂTRE". Work simply attributed to him, without a supporting signature, should be treated with suspicion.

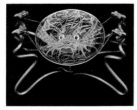

Feuillâtre's designs tend to have a strong symmetrical element: the silver snakes supporting the ring tray of this spectacular piece, *above*, are symmetrically arranged, although the decoration of the tray itself displays an asymmetrical *plique-à-jour* fish motif.

HENRI VEVER

An enamel and gold fuchsia pendant designed by Henri Vever 1889; ht 4½in/11.5cm; value code A

Identification checklist for Henri Vever jewelry
1. Is the piece finely worked, displaying a high level of craftsmanship?
2. Is it marked?
3. Is the form innovative and of botanical inspiration?
4. Is the detailing so fine as to make the piece almost a miniature sculpture?
5. Is any decoration naturalistic?
6. Does the piece contain a variety of materials?

Vever (French, 1821-1982)
Pierre Vever founded this retail and manufacturing jewelers in Metz in 1821. His son Ernest joined the company in 1848. The business moved to Paris following the German annexation of Alsace-Lorraine in 1871 and in 1881 Ernest handed over control to his sons Paul (1851-1915) and Henri (1854-1942), under whose guidance Vever became the leading Art Nouveau jewelers in Paris. The brothers combined fine technique, good form and semi-precious and precious stones to turn jewelry into a form of miniature sculpture. Their work was sculptural in a way not seen before, and is often compared to that of René Lalique although it tends to lack the inventiveness of Lalique's pieces. Vever favoured the natural forms that typify the

Art Nouveau style and took their inspiration from botanical themes. The fuchsia pendant in the main picture, designed by Henri Vever, is typical of their preoccupation with the organic. The flowerhead is articulated – an example of the minute attention to detail typical of their work. Characteristically, the design is symmetrical. Like other jewelers of the period, the Vevers used a wide variety of materials in their work: the pendant combines gold, opals, diamonds and enamelwork.

Marks
Most Vever jewelry is marked, usually with the firm's name and a serial number. The gold and enamel *collier de chien* plaque, *right*, bears the legend "Vever Paris no.1256", engraved. Alternatively, the mark could be stamped, as on the buckle, *below*.
* Some jewelry items are offered for sale in their original box and these can provide valuable information as to provenance. For example, the fuchsia pendant in the main picture still retains its original velvet and satin-lined gilt box bearing the inscription "Ane Mon Marret & Baugrand, Vever 19 Rue de la Paix 19 Paris Grand Prix Expon Univle Paris 1889" indicating that the piece was specially made for the Paris exhibition in 1889.

The gold and enamel buckle, *above*, from c.1900, displays the organic inspiration typical of Vever's decoration, with sunflowers and trailing vines. The symbolism is uncertain, although cockerels are a common

symbol for France, and the woman may represent Liberty. The piece is characteristically well chased, with good strong facial detail. The drapery is well cast and the enamelling on the cockerels is excellent. The watch face and the easel support at the back have been fitted later, turning the piece into a miniature clock. This has caused the value to suffer. The buckle was probably one of a pair originally. Most pieces appeared in limited editions, and were never mass produced.

The jewelry produced by Vever is often compared to that of René Lalique (see pp.130-1). The similarity to Lalique's work is evident in this plaque *above*, from a *collier de chien* (worn on a soft velvet collar), designed by Paul and Henri Vever in collaboration. The very fine openwork cast design is set with rose-cut diamonds and light blue *plique-à-jour* and green and orange enamelling. Interestingly, the decoration is not constrained by the design – one of the flower-heads overreaches the buckle on the left hand side of the picture. This technique tends to give perspective and a sense of depth.
* Vever commissioned several important designers, including Eugene Grasset (who was also a posterist, see p.169), Lucien Gautrait, Henri Vollet and René Rozet. Grasset's designs in particular display a strong element of symbolism.

MASRIERA BROTHERS
(Spanish, 1872-1958)
Although the firm was based in Barcelona, many of their jewelry designs show a French influence, and in particular owe something to Lalique. Use was made of *plique-à-jour* enamelwork, in which figural subjects in gold were set against shaped panels outlined with rubies on a diamanté reserve.

A silver vase designed by Josef Hoffmann
c.1905; ht 9in/24cm; value code C

Identification checklist for Josef Hoffmann's metalwork
Pierced wares
1. Is the piece of simple geometric construction?
2. Is it devoid of surface decoration?
3. Is it signed?
4. Has it been made in silver or painted metal?
5. If it has a solid cover, is there also a ball finial?

Non-pierced wares
1. Does the piece feature lobed and fluted decoration?
2. Is the surface planished (rolled or hammered smooth)?
3. Is the piece made in silver or brass?
4. Does any embossed decoration include a stylized rose?
5. Are any bases or feet spreading?
6. If a vase, is it constructed in two sections, such as a bowl and foot?

The Wiener Werkstätte (Austrian, 1903-32)

The silver and other metalwork designed by the leading members of the Wiener Werkstätte – Josef Hoffmann, Josef Maria Olbrich, and Koloman Moser – bear obvious similarities to their designs for furniture and other household objects (see pp.22-3). Common characteristics include clear lines and pure, abstract forms. Most of their work was commercially produced. Hoffmann's pieces are the most readily available.

Josef Hoffmann (1870-1956)

Hoffmann's metalwork falls into two categories – pierced and beaten. His pierced wares are purely geometric in form, like that shown *left*, and include desk stands, vases, baskets and candlesticks, all featuring pierced fretwork. Like the slender silver vase in the main picture, many vases were designed to hold glass liners. All Hoffmann pierced wares are in silver or painted metal.

The workshop's later, beaten wares were made in silver or brass, often in the form of simple ribbed vases or dishes, with a planished (hammered) surface. This silver baluster vase *above*, designed c.1910, is hammered throughout, with deep, chased flutes forming the ribs.

Josef Maria Olbrich (1867-1908)

Olbrich's style is more fluid than that of Hoffmann. His slender, tapering forms were popular in Germany, and much emulated by German manufacturers. Olbrich also produced cutlery, furniture, jewelry and posters.

Although this candelabrum, *above*, is in pewter, Olbrich also worked in silver. The curved, organic forms in low relief, are typical of his work.

Koloman Moser (1868-1918)

Like Hoffmann, Moser was influenced by Mackintosh, as well as by the English Arts and Crafts designers. His metalwork designs employed inventive forms, and he readily used planished silver or incorporated formalized friezes or panels into the decoration of his pieces. Moser's asymmetrical metal light fixtures were very unusual. Features characteristic of Moser's work include ball or semi-spherical feet, embossed or applied wood beading, combinations of metals and variously coloured woods, and iridescent glass globe shades made by Loetz (see pp.56-7).

Marks

Pieces are stamped with the "WW" trademark (see p.183) and may include the designer and/or maker's monogram.

139

WÜTTEMBERGISCHE METALLWARENFABRIK

A WMF electroplated metal photograph frame
c.1900; ht 14in/36cm; value code D/E.

Identification checklist for W.M.F. (Wüttembergische Metallwarenfabrik) art pewter
1. Does the piece include standard Art Nouveau elements, such as women with flowing garments, or trailing foliage?
2. Is it made in Continental pewter (see *below*)?
3. Is it marked?
4. Is it essentially decorative?
5. Is it shaped and possibly engraved, perhaps with stylized flowerheads?
6. Is any glass lining in clear or, more rarely, green or ruby coloured glass?

W.M.F. (Wüttembergische Metallwarenfabrik) (German, established 1880)
This metal foundry was the most successful German art pewterer of the Art Nouveau period. Designers such as Willhelm Wagenfeld took classic Art Nouveau elements – for example, women with flowing hair and garments, sinuous foliage and trailing flowers, and adapted them to commercial forms which were then mass-produced in Continental pewter, an electroplated metal alloy more similar to Britannia metal than British pewter. W.M.F. wares include vases, trophies, rose bowls and a large number of picture frames, such as the example in the main picture. The firm also produced items in glass.

Wares tend to be purely decorative rather then useful, like this pair of electroplated plaques *above*. The *repoussé* decoration shows a typical female figure with long flowing hair, surrounded by stylized poppies and sunflowers – typically Art Nouveau motifs.
* W.M.F. also produced glass claret jugs encased in pierced silver-plated decoration. In 1921 they opened a studio to produce glass liners in clear, green or ruby red glass.

Reproductions and fakes
Fakes are not known. Reproductions are suspiciously bright, with artificial black patination in crannies. Backstands on picture frames will be clearly modern and probably covered in velour, whereas originals have wooden backs and a plate and metal easel support.

Marks
W.M.F. wares made before 1914 are marked with a stork within a lozenge shape. Later wares bear just the initials "WMF".

KAYSER SOHN (German, 1885-c.1904)
J. P. Kayser & Sohn, established at Krefeld-Bochum, near Düsseldorf, was one of the first German foundries to produce art pewter, manufactured under the name Kayserzinn (Kayser pewter) from 1896. Unlike W.M.F., Kayser did not electroplate their wares, which were more akin to ordinary pewter. High standards of casting were achieved using a strong, malleable alloy of tin, copper and antimony, which gave a fine silvery shine when polished.
The majority of wares, which included ashtrays, dishes and vases, were in Jugendstil

(see p.176), although some wares show a French influence. In turn, Kayserzinn were the inspiration for Liberty's "Tudric" range (see pp.150-1).
Designers included Hugo Leven, Karl Geyer and Karl Berghoff. Forms were flowing and organic with great use of naturalistic elements.

Most Kayserzinn wares were purely decorative, although some were designed with a practical function, including ashtrays, lamps, dishes, vases and candelabra. The candelabrum *above*, has been adapted to receive electric light fittings.

ORIVIT PEWTER
Orivit pewter, produced by Rheinesche Bronzegeisserei from c.1901, is noted for its strength of design and manufacture. Wares include table mirrors, claret jugs and vases, usually with scrolling whiplash motifs which give a severe appearance. Pieces are stamped "ORIVIT". The company was bought by W.M.F.

141

MURRLE, BENNET & CO.

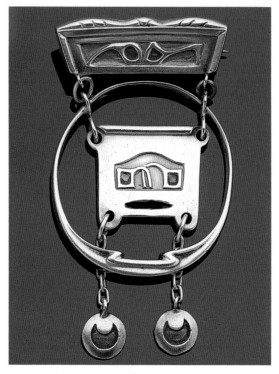

A silver-coloured, enamelled brooch designed by Patriz Huber c.1901; lgth 2in/5cm; value code D/E

Identification checklist for the jewelry designed by Theodor Fahrner for Murrle, Bennet & Co.
1. Are motifs geometric or based on stylized plants, animals or birds?
2. Is use made of enamelling in peacock green and blue, or semi-precious stones?
3. Is the piece marked?
4. Is the form organic?
5. Is any decoration openwork?

Murrle, Bennet & Co. (Anglo-German, 1884-1914)
Ernst Murrle, a German jeweler, and Mr Bennet, established this Anglo-German agency in London, retailing low-priced jewelry in gold and silver, including many designs produced in Pforzheim, Germany by Theodor Fahrner, a school friend of Murrle's.

Theodor Fahrner (German, 1868-1928)
Fahrner, considered the most original jeweler in Pforzheim, produced probably the first art jewelry available on a mass-produced scale. As they did not incorporate real gems, pieces did not need to be inspected and could be ordered by catalogue.

Fahrner's own work tends to be figurative, abstract or semi-organic in form, with highly-stylized decoration. He was fond of bird motifs; the silver and enamel pin *above* is typical of his designs. Webbed wing motifs often appear on Fahrner pieces.

Fahrner's jewelry
The firm made inexpensive pieces in silver or low-carat gold, set with enamelwork, semi-precious stones, mother-of-pearl or glass. Pieces, such as the pendant in the main picture, made from silver-coloured metal and enamel, have little intrinsic value. This example was designed by Patriz Huber, the most prolific of Fahrner's designers. Despite the attachments to this piece, most of Huber's work is simple, with dull surfaces and subdued stones or enamelling. Fahrner's jewelry appears hand-made, but was in fact made using Liberty's methods of mass-production. Some pieces are cast with simulated rivets for decorative effect.

Several designers worked for Fahrner within the same abstract, organic style. The pendant *above*, designed by Franz Bohres, is in the Secessionist style, probably influenced by Joseph Maria Olbrich, a Vienna Secessionist who worked for Fahrner (among others). The geometric feel created by the vertical bars and triangles is typically Germanic and common in Fahrner jewelry. The openwork and simple form are also typical.
* Some pieces were designed as part of a set.
* Attribution to a designer will increase the value of a piece.

Marks
Most pieces bear a stamped mark, either "MB" or "MB & Co.". Of all the pieces shown here, only the Bohres pendant does not have a designer's monogram. Most pieces should also have the collaborator's mark.

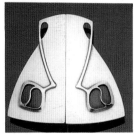

The silver-coloured metal and enamel buckle *above*, designed for Fahrner by Albrecht Holbein c.1900, is stamped with Holbein's mark and the word "Geschutzt" (meaning: copyright); each element is numbered "VII".

Murrle Bennet and Liberty
Fahrner's work was similar in many respects to Liberty's "Cymric" range (see pp.146-9). Liberty sold some Fahrner jewelry and a few recorded Liberty designs also appear in Murrle Bennet catalogues. It was always assumed that Murrle Bennet copied Liberty, but it now seems likely that Murrle Bennet produced modern jewelry first, and may have supplied Liberty with designs.
* Some enamelled silver pendants designed by Archibald Knox (see pp.146-9) were made by Murrle Bennet and bear that factory's mark.

GEORG JENSEN

A silver tureen designed by Georg Jensen 1908; lgth 12in/30cm; value code B

Identification checklist for Jensen silverware
1. Is the form relatively simple or traditional, but embellished with applied naturalistic motifs, such as roses?
2. Do any feet incorporate tendril and pod motifs?
3. Is the piece silver?
4. Is it hallmarked?
5. Are surfaces smooth, or perhaps lightly planished?
6. Is any applied decoration *repoussé* (see below)?

Georg Jensen (Danish, 1866-1935)
The designs produced in the early years of the 20thC by the Danish silversmith Georg Jensen have a timeless quality, and remain in production even today. Jensen opened his Copenhagen workshop in 1904 to produce silver tablewares and a range of brooches and necklaces. Many of Jensen's designs, particularly the very extensive range of cutlery, were revolutionary. The tureen in the main picture is exceptional in that it is entirely hand-made; most of the firm's products combined hand and machine production. Jensen's designs enjoyed great popularity in Scandinavia, and large quantities were exported to the United States.
* Most designs were standard productions. Jensen produced only a few commissioned pieces.

Decoration
Georg Jensen's designs typically feature finely sculpted decorative motifs drawn from nature. The decoration is generally applied, often to a fairly simply-shaped vessel; this would have been unusual for a period when the majority of designers attempted to integrate form and decoration. Jensen favoured the rose as a decorative motif, and had a fondness for pod and tendril forms, which he often used for finials and supports.
* The applied decoration on much Jensen silver is *repoussé* (a form of metalwork decoration produced in relief by hammering the reverse side); the petals on the tureen in the main picture were made using this technique.
* Some pieces incorporate ivory handles. Aside from their decorative function, these also act as insulators.

MAISON BOUCHERON
(French, 1858-present)

This Parisian jewelry manufacturer, founded by Frederick Boucheron (1830-1902), had branches in Biarritz, London and New York and produced designs mainly for the French and American markets. Like Jensen, the firm successfully adapted shapes and motifs popular during the late 18thC and early 19thC to the modern Art Nouveau style. The firm also combined both hand and machine production. It specialized in jewelry set with precious stones; the majority of designs are opulent and heavily embellished with diamonds.

In the years immediately following the establishment of his Copenhagen workshop, Jensen was by no means responsible for all the firm's designs. The modernistic sugar caster, *above*, made of silver, amber, coral and malachite, was designed by the Danish architect Anton Rosen (1858-1928) and produced by the Jensen workshop c.1908. This particular combination of designer and producer makes the piece especially desirable for collectors.
* This caster is unusual in its combination of silver and other materials. The form itself is also distinctive, and represents a departure from the more characteristically restrained designs produced by the firm in this period.
* Like the tureen in the main picture, the surface of this piece has been lightly hammered. On most Jensen designs, the surface is left smooth.

Decoration is of very high quality, exemplified by the sculpted leaves and roses on the tea service *above*. As here, it is restricted to handles, spouts and lids; surfaces are often planished. Accentuated handles, which on the teapot feature ivory insulation bars, are also a feature of some French porcelain.
* A gilt interior, visible on the cream jug, is a sign of a high-quality piece.

Marks
All the firm's designs are stamped either "JENSEN" or with the initials "GJ", perhaps entwined. *Below* are three possible variations.

Marks
All Boucheron silverware should bear a French hallmark. Most pieces are stamped, either with "BOUCHERON PARIS" or simply the initial "B" *below*.

LIBERTY: CYMRIC 1

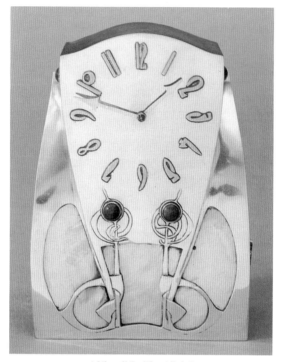

A Liberty & Co. "Cymric" clock
1903; ht 9²/₃in/24.5cm; value code B

Identification checklist for Cymric silver and metalwork designed by Archibald Knox for Liberty & Co.
1. Does the piece display Celtic-inspired motifs?
2. Is it marked with the trade name "Cymric"?
3. Is it embellished with peacock blue/green enamels?
4. Is the form innovative?
5. Is the piece inset with turquoise, lapis lazuli, or similar semi-precious stone cabochons?
6. Is the hallmark for 1900 or later?
7. If a clock, is the chapter ring applied in copper or enamelled in white against blue and green?

Liberty & Co. (English, 1875-present)
Arthur Lasenby Liberty founded this famous London retail firm in 1875, initially for the sale of British-made goods and imported Oriental art and fabrics. In the 1880s the firm began to commission art fabric designs and

to produce Arts and Crafts-style furniture, and by 1900 was widely regarded as the arbiter of taste in interior decoration. In 1899 it launched its "Cymric" silverware range. In 1901, Liberty & Co. (Cymric) Ltd. was formed, in conjunction with the Birmingham silver firm of W. H. Haseler.

Archibald Knox (English, 1864-1933)

Archibald Knox was the most important of the designers called upon by Liberty to produce designs for the Cymric range. He produced more than 400 designs for the range, as well as some "Tudric" pewter (see pp.150-1).

Knox was born and educated on the Isle of Man, and his observation of Celtic remains there was the underlying influence on his choice of decoration. The ornate elements are easily recognized, and often incorporate spear-headed entrelac symbols, a form of interlaced decoration drawn from ancient jewelry. Such motifs are clearly visible on the mantel clock in the main picture. On this piece, the design is enhanced by the use of enamels and applied cabochons (polished, unfaceted stones), both features associated with medieval Limoges enamel work. Knox used enamels to highlight the entrelacs, with blue-green being the colour most commonly used.

The copper numerals were not peculiar to Liberty, but the combination of copper and silver was uncommon. Copper was widely used in this period, but more often against gold. Liberty did not baulk at using or combining non-precious or semi-precious metals.

The clock *above* has turquoise and inlaid mother-of-pearl decoration, both characteristic of Knox.
* Mechanisms should preferably be in working order. However, it is unwise to replace movements, even where they are not working.

Knox was particularly adept at adapting conventional forms. The novel thumb rest and hinged handle on this tankard, *above*, enliven an otherwise standard form. The enamelling is in the typical blue-green colour.

Clocks

Knox's clock forms were usually highly original and architectural, often with a tapering body and perhaps with an overhanging pediment. The mantel clock in the main picture, attributed to Knox, is one of the most innovative of his many designs.

The tobacco box *above* combines a modern function with medieval motifs. The architectural form, overhanging lid and wire mount echo the Guild of Handicraft (see pp.154-5). The restrained decoration includes panels of shagreen (green-stained sharkskin).

Knox's Cymric chalices did not feature religious motifs, and were probably made for domestic use or as presentation cups. Some, such as the example *above*, had multiple supports entwined with tendril-type wirework.

Attribution
Liberty's designers did not sign their work and Knox is the only one whose pieces can be attributed with any certainty, as many of his designs survive.

The silver chalice, *above*, might have been the work of either Knox or Reginald (Rex) Silver (1897-1965), one of the first designers to work on the Cymric range. However, the lack of Celtic-derived motifs, the

untypical combination of stones and the too delicate and fluid style of the piece suggests that it is more likely to be by Silver.
* Chalices usually stand on a disc-shaped base, sometimes with a slightly raised centre.
* Decoration tends to be limited to the support, with the bowl left plain.

Traditional shapes
The relatively traditional form of the enamel vase, *below*, was common on porcelain throughout the early 19thC, but the decoration is highly individual. Knox managed to maintain a balance between design and form and his work was always well-proportioned.

The distinctive tree design, the entwined stems and honesty-type flowers of the vase *above* are typical of the work of Archibald Knox. The blue-green coloured enamel used to decorate the flowers and tendrils is also characteristic (see pp.150-1).
* Knox's output was larger than that of other silver designers, and object for object, his work is the most prized. However, the price of a piece will depend first on the object itself, rather than its designer.
* Like many Cymric wares, this vase is stamped with a shape number, "Rd 467167", as well as the maker's mark. Most pieces also bear a Birmingham hallmark which will always be dated later than 1900 (when the range was introduced). The name "CYMRIC" usually appears.

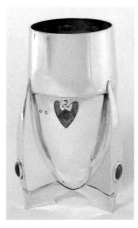

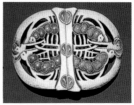

The enamelled buckle, *above*, displays characteristic symmetry. Other elements consistent with the work of King include:
* the planished surface
* the swallows around the edges of the buckle, evidence of King's fondness for stylized bird motifs
* the bright, peacock blue-green enamelwork on the stylized flowerheads.

The form of a piece is generally reflected in its decoration: the enamelled hearts and simple entrelacs that embellish the vase *above* complement the form, although the bullet shape is the focus of attention. The design is very innovative and would have been avant garde for its day.

Pendants
Pendants were very popular during the Art Nouveau period, and tended to be particularly sculptural in form, with the emphasis on design rather than value. As a jewelry designer, King was fond of an elaborate, multiple-type construction.

Knox was a prolific jeweler, with a fondness for brooches and buckles, such as the example *above*. The surface has been "distressed" (artificially aged), a common effect on Knox's jewelry. Other examples have colour enamelling giving a jewel-like appearance.

Jessie M. King (Scottish, 1876-1949)
King, a prominent member of the Glasgow School (see pp.28-9), produced some of the most exciting jewelry in the Cymric range. Enamelwork features on some designs, notably in the form of peacock blue and green enamel flowerheads. Her silver tends to have a planished (finely hammered) surface, and her designs were often symmetrical.

Of Liberty jewelry, it is the work of Fred Partridge (1877-1942) that most shows a French influence. The Partridge necklace *above* features moonstones and dragonflies along the chain, both also typical of Lalique (see pp.130-1). Partridge, an important jewelry designer in his own right, produced a large number of items carved from horn, including hairslides. Pieces not produced for Liberty are marked "PARTRIDGE".

LIBERTY: TUDRIC

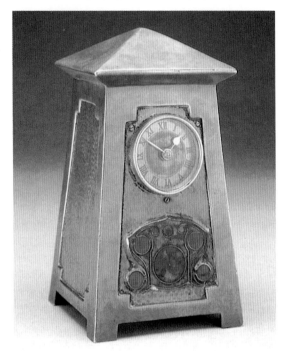

*A Liberty pewter and enamel clock
c.1905; ht 7in/18.5cm; value code D*

Identification checklist for Liberty & Co.'s "Tudric" pewter

1. Has use been made of Celtic-inspired strapwork, entwined leaves of honesty or entrelac motifs?
2. Does the piece rely on colourful enamel cabochons rather than semi-precious stones?
3. Is it marked "TUDRIC"?
4. Is the design innovative?
5. Is there a four-figure shape number, possibly with an "0" prefix?

Tudric wares
Until 1902, Liberty retailed Kayser-Zinn wares (see pp.140-1) and other German art pewter. Following the success of these ranges and of the Cymric silver range, Arthur Liberty saw the opportunity to produce similar wares in the less expensive pewter. In so doing, he helped to revive the pewter industry,

which had declined as pewter tavern wares were largely replaced by mass-produced glassware. The first Tudric wares were made in 1903 by the Birmingham firm, W. H. Haseler & Co., who were already making the Cymric range. Mainly for domestic use, they often incorporate decorative enamelwork, as does the clock *above*.

Designs and decoration
Liberty employed several of the Cymric designers to work on the Tudric range; indeed, many Tudric designs were inspired by the earlier Cymric wares.

Some Tudric designs have a traditional, architectural form: the tapering sides and overhanging top of the pewter and enamel clock in the main picture are consistent with traditional forms. Others were innovative, and decoration often verged on the avant-garde.

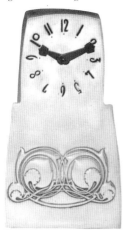

Some of the earlier Tudric clocks have a distinctive enamelled dial created using a quick process whereby a shape was impressed into the metal and the sunken area then flooded with enamel. Entire dials could be enamelled in this way, or simply small areas of the design. The black, recessed numerals on the clock *above* were produced using this process. The clock was designed by Archibald Knox in c.1902. His characteristic Celtic-inspired entrelac motifs (see pp.146-7), seen here on the case of the clock, are typically more complex than on his earlier Cymric wares.

Knox was the most prominent designer of Tudric wares, as he had been with the earlier Cymric range. Other designs were by Oliver Baker (1856-1939) and Bernard Cuzner (1877-1956).
* As on Cymric clocks, the hands should be original. They are often distinctive and are sometimes even enamelled.

* Liberty faced a large amount of competition from Sheffield and Midlands metalwork shops, but little which is worthy of specific mention. Most products tended to have hammered surfaces and simple forms, and often have ebonized wood handles.
* The Tudric range includes some rare cigarette boxes decorated with inset rectangular panels enamelled with landscapes and signed by Fleetwood Charles Varley, one of the few artists to sign their work.

Although some Tudric forms were borrowed from the earlier Cymric wares, many, like the inkstand *above*, were unique to the Tudric range. Enamelled wares command a premium, although small losses of enamelling, such as that on the circular decoration in the front right hand corner of this piece will slightly reduce value.

The enamelled cake basket *above*, from 1905, is stamped with the number "0357", a stock or shape number. Three-figure or lower numbers, usually preceded by an "0", indicate an early date. Some designs were reissued in the 1920s; these bear a five-figure number.
* Some Tudric wares may also be stamped "ENGLISH PEWTER" and "MADE BY LIBERTY & CO.".

Later wares
After 1918, the range declined in quality. Later pieces have a heavy emphasis on simulated hammered surfaces and little, if any, enamelwork. Production ceased c.1938.

WILLIAM HUTTON & SONS

A silver mirror designed by Kate Harris for Huttons
1902; lgth 11in/28.5cm; value code D

Identification checklist for silver designed by Kate Harris
1. Is the decoration figural, or does it feature honesty flowers or lilies?
2. If figural, does it feature a profiled portrait of a Quaker-type woman set against a halo-like medallion?
3. Is the form slightly out of the ordinary, or treated unusually, yet essentially traditional?
4. Is the piece hallmarked and signed?
5. Is the surface of any reserve granular in quality?

William Hutton and Sons (English, 1800-1923)
Founded in Birmingham by William Hutton, this firm produced both useful and ornamental wares in fine quality silver, silver plate, Britannia metal, pewter and copper. From 1887 to 1914, under the director-ship of Thomas Swaffield-Brown, Hutton's mass-produced some influential Art Nouveau wares in enamelled copper and silver. Much of their silverware of this period was made to the designs of Kate Harris (see *opposite*). Most other designers are so far anonymous.

Kate Harris (English, active c.1890-1910)

Kate Harris began designing for Huttons in 1901, and fast became their foremost designer. She made useful and decorative wares in a distinctive style that displayed her individual interpretation of Art Nouveau. Her best work strikes a balance between decoration and form, achieved by combining inventive shapes with stylized figurative work. She mainly produced objects for a lady's dressing table, some of which were exhibited at the Paris Exposition in 1900.

Motifs

Harris's figurative subjects are generally female with a distinctive, Quaker-like appearance, suggested by a close-fitting Dutch-style hat. Most have a curl protruding from beneath the cap, and are shown in profile against a halo-like medallion, such as the example on the mirrorback in the main picture. The religious significance of this particular piece is heightened by the two lilies that flank the figure, a symbolic allusion to the Virgin Mary.

The casket *above* is not definitely by Harris, but has been attributed to her on the basis of the honesty flower decoration and the renaissance-type scroll-form cartouche – both of which were typical of her work. The casket is basically of traditional form, but with innovative embossing.

* Harris often gave the reserve areas within her designs an almost granular, finely pitted orange peel texture. On the mirror the effect is to make the subject appear in relief. This texture was achieved by machine, treating the silver as a plastic material or fabric.
* The casket will be lined with velvet inside and was probably used for jewelry.
* The cartouche lends itself to inscription.
* Harris designed several photograph frames, one of which incorporates colour enamelled stylized flower and stem decoration above a heart motif.
* Handles are an important feature of many Harris pieces: a coffee set of 1902 exhibits accentuated loop and wrapover handles. A sporting cup by her has elaborately pierced handles. The sinuous whiplash handles on a silver bowl liner extend from the rim to the base.

Marks

Harris was purely a designer and consequently did not sign her wares; all her designs were made by William Hutton and Sons and bear the Hutton's mark (see *below*), and a London hallmark.

The design of the blue glass bottle *above* is strong and the decoration of trailing ivy leaves typically Art Nouveau. The glass lining, which was probably produced by the London glasshouse, James Powell and Sons (see pp.62-3), is original, which will increase the value.

Collecting

The value of Hutton's wares will be dictated by the individual piece. The work of Kate Harris commands a premium. There are no known fakes or imitations.

BRITISH ARTS GUILDS

*A Guild of Handicraft cloak clasp
c.1902; wdth 5in/14cm; value code C*

Identification checklist for Guild of Handicraft silver and jewelry
1. Is the piece hand-made?
2. Is it marked?
3. Is the form original (and possibly derived from nature)?
4. Is there any beaten decoration?
5. Is there any enamel work?
6. Are there any inset cabochons or semi-precious stones?
7. Are there friezes with embossed or pierced flowers and leaves?

British Arts Guilds
The guild system developed in England during the later years of Queen Victoria's reign, and brought together designers and craftsmen determined to produce beautiful objects using handcrafting processes that dated back to medieval times.

The Guild of Handicraft (British, 1888-1908)
This guild, founded by Charles Robert Ashbee (1863-1942), was notable for the production of superb silverware fashioned by craftsmen who, until the Guild's formation, had not worked in this medium. Ashbee himself was the Guild's most fertile and influential designer. The Guild sought to produce objects of original form which took their inspiration only from nature. Particular use was made of wirework – for example in the creation of elongated handles. The ideals of the Guild failed as a result of competition from the imported jewelry made by the

German firm, Murrle Bennet (see pp.142-3), amongst others, and by the silver and pewter wares retailed by Liberty & Co (see pp.146-151), which, despite being machine-made, appeared hand-crafted.
* Other guilds included the Artificer's Guild, founded by Nelson Dawson and Edward Spencer, and the Century Guild, one of whose founders was Arthur H. Mackmurdo.

Decoration
Guild pieces featured naturalistic decoration, often in the form of embossed or pierced friezes of flowers and leaves, with figural decoration restricted to terminals or finials. The silver cloak clasp in the main picture, designed by Ashbee, features amethyst and turquoise cabochons (smoothly polished, unfaceted gems), as well as enamelling, both favourite forms of decoration with Guild designers.
* Ashbee's designs were often carried out by other craftsmen.

established an enamelling school in 1904. He helped to found the Birmingham Guild of Handicraft and inspired contemporaries such as Nelson and Edith Dawson and Phoebe Traquair.

Fisher's silverware, which consists mainly of plaques, often depicts Celtic-inspired entrelac motifs and influenced Liberty's Cymric range of silverware (see pp.146-9).

Marks
Most of Fisher's designs bear his stamped initials. The silver cross and panel below is also dated (1899) and bears the remains of an exhibition label inscribed "The Countess Grey/Howick Lebury Northumberland/Enamel by Alexander Fisher/1899", indicating that it was designed by Fisher to a commission from Earl or Countess Grey.

The hammered silver cup and cover, *above*, also designed by Ashbee, takes the medieval-inspired form of a chalice. However, the decoration is typically Art Nouveau, and incorporates a chased band of leaves around the rim. Certain features suggest that the piece was hand-crafted:
* the mother-of-pearl cabochon on top of the openwork finial lies at an angle, indicating that it was not mechanically set.
* the lid is not flush with the rim of the cup.

Marks
Most wares are stamped with the firm's initials, *below, left*. The individual designers and makers were not usually credited, except Ashbee, whose pieces may bear his initials "CRA", stamped (*below, right*). John Pearson, another Guild silversmith, stamped some of his work.

Alexander Fisher (English, 1864-1936)
Alexander Fisher is regarded as the greatest British enameller, and the one responsible for taking enamelling to the heights achieved at Limoges during the Renaissance. He founded his own London workshop, where he

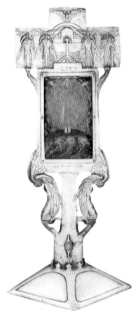

Fisher's plaques were often set into elaborate mounts or frames such as the silver cross *above*. Many had a religious subject: this piece depicts Christ rising above three sleeping mortals. The frame is supported by two kneeling angels, while another four rise above the scene.

GORHAM CORPORATION

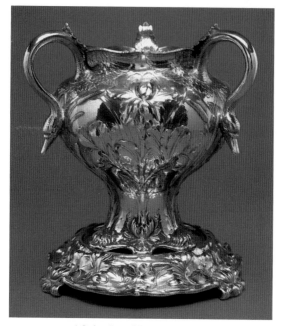

A Gorham "martelé" silver vase on stand
c.1900; ht 13in/33cm; value code B

Identification checklist for Gorham "martelé" silver
1. Does the surface have a lightly hammered texture?
2. Are any decorative elements typically Art Nouveau?
3. Is the piece marked with the "Martelé" trademark (see *below*)?
4. Is the form fluid and the contours smooth?
5. Is the piece entirely hand-made?

**Gorham Corporation
(American, 1813-present)**
This Rhode Island firm, the
largest 19thC American silver
producer, used mechanical
methods to make fine silver
wares. In 1868 Gorham adopted
the Sterling standard for silver
(925 parts of silver per 1000),
replacing the coin standard (only
900 parts per 1000), and by 1891
were using the Britannia standard
(950 parts per 1000).

"Martelé" wares
Between 1891 and 1910, Gorham
produced their "martelé" line of
silverware. Hand-made to the

Britannia standard, martelé is
now the most collectable of all
American Art Nouveau
silverware. The wares tend to be
thick and heavily gauged, with
smooth contours and a lightly
hammered (planished) surface.
Many martelé wares feature
repoussé or chased decoration;
hollowares, such as the vase on a
stand in the main picture, tend to
be particularly heavily chased.
The influence of the Rococo can
still be clearly seen in the
elaborate decoration of this vase,
but the waterlily and cat tail
motifs are typical of Art
Nouveau, as are the handles.

Collecting

Smaller, early wares and unusual forms are more sought after than later wares. However, output was small and martelé is rare today. The Gorham Corporation mass-produced a large amount of Art Nouveau silver at around the same time, which is of little collectable interest.

The martelé vase *above* is a later piece, dating from around 1910. The fluid form is typically Art Nouveau, as are the floral motifs with trailing stems, which create a strong vertical emphasis. The decoration is not as heavily *repoussé* as on the vase in the main picture. Some Gorham wares were relatively large; this vase is over 15in (38cm) high.

UNGER BROTHERS (1872-c.1910)

Founded by five brothers, Unger's impressive range of Art Nouveau silver, produced from 1890 and designed mainly by Emma L. Dickinson, includes dressing table sets, match-holders and jewelry. Pieces tend to be heavily chased or *repoussé*, with floral or figural decoration. The most sought-after wares have unusual forms and display female or American Indian images. The jewelry is especially collectable. Common items, such as hairbrushes, are of little value.

HERMAN MARCUS (American, estab. 1900)

Marcus was probably the finest American jeweler of the Art Nouveau period. A former employee of Charles Tiffany, he established Marcus and Co. in New York in 1900, making jewelry and cufflinks in both gold and platinum, decorated with gemstones and enamel. The most outstanding pieces are the extraordinary floral jewels made in gold and *plique-à-jour* enamel.

This example *above*, from c.1900, displays Marcus' virtuosity as a jeweler. The influence of French Art Nouveau jewelers, particularly René Lalique (see pp.130-1) is clear in this piece, although Marcus' jewelry tends to be more delicate, lightweight and fragile.

Marks

The distinctive anchor mark *below, left* appears on most Gorham wares, with perhaps a serial number and a stamp confirming the silver standard.

Most Unger wares bear the monogram *above, right*; sometimes only the "U" appears. * Other notable silversmiths, such as Black Starr and Frost, the Alvin Manufacturing Company and Simons Brothers, maintained a conventional approach to design and little of their work is of significant value.

DIRK VAN ERP

A copper and mica table lamp by Dirk van Erp
c.1911; ht 15in/39.5cm; value code B

Identification checklist for Van Erp metalwork

1. Is the object made of hammered copper?
2. Does it have a mottled patina with reddish-brown areas?
3. Is the form simple and of Japanese inspiration?
4. Are the standards of metalworking and design extremely high?
5. Are all methods of construction, including rivets and seams, visible and integral to the design?
6. Does the object show evidence of being entirely hand-made?
7. If a lamp, does the shade feature panels of amber-coloured mica?

Dirk Van Erp (Dutch, 1860-1953)
The son of a Dutch coppersmith, Van Erp moved to California in 1886. In 1908 he opened *The Copper Shop* in Oakland, where he made decorative copper wares finished with hammered surfaces and a rich reddish brown patina. He moved to San Francisco in 1910, and expanded his range to include vases and desk items, including table lamps with mica shades. His work is scarce, and almost unknown outside the United States and Canada, where the value of his wares has soared in recent years, in line with the general increase in demand for fine American arts and crafts.

Van Erp rejected new-fangled production methods and worked in a simple style referred to as "Mission" style, which had its roots in the Prairie School (see pp.36-7). His pieces were simple in form and design and hand-made using traditional techniques and tools. His work displays standards of design and production comparable to the best medieval examples. Rivets and seams tend to be visible, or even integral to the design. On the table lamp in the main picture, the trumpet-shaped battens of the shade echo the style of the base, and the rivets on both the battens and the arms

act as decoration on an otherwise simple piece. Van Erp's table lamps are among his most collectable pieces. Most are in the same hammered, reddish-brown copper with shades panelled in mottled mica sheets. Forms vary; bases can be trumpet-shaped, or may take the form of mushrooms, miniature milk churns or bullets. The pod-form base of the copper piano lamp *above*, made c.1910, is very unusual and would command a particularly high price at auction.
* Van Erp signed most of his designs with either his full name or monogram beneath a windmill device.

THE ROYCROFTERS
(American, 1895-1938)
Founded in East Aurora by Elbert Hubbard (1856-1917), this community produced simple, well-made mahogany and fumed oak furniture in the Mission style, as well as textiles, hammered metalwork, books and lighting.

Although based on the English Arts and Crafts style, their work was distinctively American and became known as Aurora Colonial furniture. The metalwork of Karl Kipp, a designer in the Secessionist style and director of the metal workshops from 1908, is very collectable.

Wrought-iron wares were first produced in 1899 and included vases, light fittings and andirons (rests for burning logs in an open fireplace), such as those shown *right*, in the shape of seahorses. These were designed by William Walter Denislow.

Manufacture Royale, Corsets, *by T. Privat Livemont, c.1897*

By the end of the 19thC, increased industrialization and the subsequent need for advertising had led to vast growth in the importance of the poster as a means of communication. Letter-press was replaced by modern techniques, such as lithography, whereby an image is drawn in crayon onto a lithographic stone – a soft limestone. Acid, poured over the stone, etches away uncovered areas, leaving a raised image which is inked and applied to paper. Each colour is done in turn. The stone could be sanded down and reused, making this a cheaper method than engraving or etching.

The French dominated lithography. Jules Chéret (see pp.166-7), among others, covered *fin de siècle* Paris in striking posters, to the extent that a law was introduced to prevent their being posted. These now serve as a fascinating pictorial record of the times, as does the work of Toulouse-

Lautrec (see pp.164-5), whose posters of Parisian lowlife are probably the best known of the period. Posters were never as popular in Britain, nor are they collected to the same extent as in Europe and the United States.

All posters were commercial – the example shown here recommends a brand of corset. The figure is an archetypical Art Nouveau woman with flowing hair, surrounded by floral motifs and billowing drapery, a style introduced by Alphonse Mucha (see pp.162-3). Elsewhere in Europe, the artists of the Austrian Secession (see pp.172-3) designed boldly geometric posters with simple precision-designed lettering to advertise exhibitions mounted by the movement.

In the United States, the work of Maxfield Parrish (see pp.174-5) was perhaps the best example of American Art Nouveau applied to commercial art; as well as mass-produced graphic art he also designed covers for magazines such as *Harper's*, *Life*, and *Scribners Magazine*.

Although posters were produced in large numbers, especially in Britain they were never designed to be kept or collected, hence their limited availability. Paper shortages during two World Wars led to official paper calls which destroyed many posters, as did the dumping of old stock by merging printing companies.

Several points may affect the value of a poster. Among lesser artists, the quality of graphics becomes the deciding factor: a stunning image will be valuable even if anonymous. Condition is vital, although the value of a poster by a prominent artist will not be dramatically affected by bad condition. Posters in pristine condition command a premium. Some were personalized by overprinting – for example, a firm might add a calendar. This does not always devalue a piece but purists may prefer the clean print. A number of catalogue terms apply specifically to posters. "Loss" refers to a missing piece; these are crucial, and should be replaced. A "tear" can be prevented from ripping further with the use of acid-free tape. Sellotape or dry mounting (sticking the poster to a backing board) should not be used: they are damaging and irreversible. Care should be taken in buying any backed poster; ensure the glue used is vegetable based and hence, being water soluble, reversible. If stuck to hardboard with non-reversible glue, it is worth having it removed by a poster specialist. Once removed it should be rebacked with japan paper or linen using reversible glue. When framing, glaze with plexiglass rather than glass. This is lighter to hang and less dangerous should it crack. "Foxing" refers to a type of acidic mould. This can be removed by bleaching, but this is bound to fade the colours. Avoid posters that are badly "light stained" (faded by exposure to strong light), or have prominent blemishes. No restoration should ever be tried, however easy it might seem: the work should always be given to a specialist.

The colour blocks on reproductions are formed of hundreds of little dots and are fairly easily distinguished from a lithograph, which has solid colours and crayon lines.

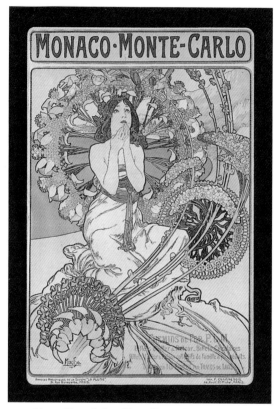

Monaco Monte-Carlo, *a lithographic poster by Alphonse Mucha*
1897; ht 43in/109cm; value code: B/C

Identification checklist for the posters of Alphonse Mucha
1. Does the poster depict a woman clad in diaphanous robes, or a subject in theatrical costume?
2. Does she have long flowing hair or hair *en chignon* (twisted into a bun)?
3. Does she have an ethereal quality?
4. Is the design busy?
5. Is gilding included in any decoration?
6. Is the poster signed by Mucha and the printer?

Alphonse Mucha (Czech, 1860-1939)
Mucha's dramatic flowing style has made his name synonymous with the Art Nouveau movement. He worked as a scene painter in Vienna and came to prominence in the 1890s when the great actress Sarah Bernhardt commissioned him to design posters for her, and later, costumes, jewelry and stage sets. Most of his collectable work was executed between 1890 and 1910.

Motifs

The subject of *Monaco Monte-Carlo*, in the main picture, is typical of Mucha's better known figures, with her scant clothing and long, flowing hair; he also depicted women with more complicated drapery and hair *en chignon*. Most are reminiscent of Sarah Bernhardt, although he used other models in some sittings, as the actress had only one leg. The flower garlands symbolize the wheels of the train linked by rail lines. The lettering was done by Mucha himself. Mucha's designs tend to involve many decorative elements, such as exotic flora, jewels or diadems. Figures are often framed in this way with arches or lettering (see *below right*).

Mucha produced calendars and albums of decorative motifs, containing life sketches and designs for jewelry, furniture and floral panels, such as the lilies shown *above*. The albums contain 72 plates and are usually complete, although single sheets turn up from time to time.

Signature

Mucha's posters are nearly always ''signed in the block'', meaning as a part of the design. He sometimes countersigned the completed poster by hand.

Condition

Mucha's work is rarely in perfect condition: colours and gilding tend to wear. Tears are not crucial, but damage to the central image can reduce the value.

Authenticity

The poster in the main picture is relatively large and, as a lithograph stone could not be made to such large dimensions, will have been printed on two sheets of paper. Posters of this size are very difficult to fake successfully: for this reason the majority of fakes tend to be of the smaller designs that can be produced on one stone.

Mucha produced several versions of some posters, perhaps varying some of the details. The piece *above*, announcing the performance of de Musset's *Lorenzaccio* with Sarah Bernhardt in 1896, appeared in at least two sizes using different colours. Some versions omit the garter on the figure's right leg or vary other small details.

* The arch framing the subject is typical.

HENRI DE TOULOUSE-LAUTREC

La Revue Blanche, *a lithograph by Henri de Toulouse-Lautrec 1895; 37in x 51½in/93.5cm x 130cm; value code A/B*

Identification checklist for Toulouse-Lautrec posters
1. Does the poster advertise a particular event or establishment?
2. If a promotional piece, does it advertise a theatre or perhaps a retailer or an exhibition?
3. Does it depict Paris low-life?
4. Does the paper appear thin, uneven and very fragile?
5. If a female subject, is she ugly?
6. Is the lettering style simple, almost haphazard?
7. Is the poster signed?

Henri de Toulouse-Lautrec (French, 1864-1901)
Born an aristocrat, Toulouse-Lautrec suffered an accident as a boy which left him a dwarf. He frequented the seedier areas of Paris, including such theatres and nightclubs around Montmartre and Pigalle as *Le Moulin Rouge*. He is best known for posters depicting Parisian nightlife, but also promoted exhibitions and retailers and worked for various periodicals. His most usual

subjects were theatrical women, often ugly in appearance – the woman in the poster in the main picture, Missia Natanson, the wife of the *Revue Blanche's* co-director, is relatively attractive when compared to other Lautrec figures.

The proofing process

Proofs, or trial impressions made at an early stage in the printing process, lack the lettering bearing the name of the establishment, show, and so on. They are rare and valuable and sought after by both print and poster collectors. Contemporary catalogues *(catalogues raisonnés)*, should record the number of copies made at each stage of proofing. Lautrec often included amusing little sketches on the stone, which were erased from the final version.

Fakes

Toulouse-Lautrec's posters have been faked, copied and reproduced more than any other posterist or artist of the age.

The poster *above*, called *Le Divan Japonais*, advertises a theatre of that name, and depicts Yvette Gilbert on stage, watched by the actress Jane Avril and Edouard Dujardin, the critic. First printed in 1893, it was reissued in 1904 with subtle differences – for example, the black of Gilbert's corset was more solid. The Swiss produced a series of innocent reproduction lithographs in the 1950s, clearly marked as such and bearing a distinctive stamp. However, this stamp is sometimes soaked off, or hidden by being backed with linen.

Original or reproduction?

Several checks can be made: genuine posters were done on the stone, colour by colour, and a thin band of overlapping colours can usually be seen along the bottom edge. This colour difference is evened out on lithographs and photographic reproductions, leaving a single band of colour. Good quality paper indicates a "fake". Colours should be checked against a known original as they can seldom be precisely reproduced.

Condition

Posters were dispatched folded, so fold marks are common, but may be more distinct on some works than on others.

On the poster *above*, entitled *Reine de Joie*, the distinct fold mark cuts across the image, a fact which is obviously undesirable. However, some posters have been trimmed and, as this seriously reduces the value, it is important to know the size of the original, which should be recorded in the *catalogues raisonnés*.

Collecting point

There is an instance where it is acceptable to "marry" parts of different posters. Lautrec's most famous poster, advertising *Le Moulin Rouge* and known as *La Goulue*, comes in three sections. The lower two sections are rare but can be found; however, the top, lettered section is extremely rare, and a marriage between a top section and the lower sections is acceptable.

JULES CHÉRET

Le Figaro, *a lithographic poster by Jules Chéret*
1904; 23 x 32in/58.5 x 81.25cm; value code D

Identification checklist for the posters of Jules Chéret
1. Is the subject female?
2. Is the composition lively?
3. Are outlines simplified, with a minimum of detail?
4. Is the subject very much in the foreground, against a shadowy background?
5. Is the poster signed, and perhaps dated?
6. Does it bear the name of the printer?

Jules Chéret (French, 1836-1932)
Although he was essentially a commercial artist, Chéret is recognized today as the father of the poster. His exuberant designs perfectly reflected the mood of *fin-de-siècle* Paris.

Posters had previously been produced using the letterpress method, whereby designs were printed from a raised, inked surface. By drawing his designs directly onto stone, Chéret developed the use of lithography (see pp.160-1) as a creative medium. He began to produce lithographic posters in 1858.

A seven-year stay in England introduced him to new methods of mass production using coloured blocks, and in 1866 he began to produce posters on his own press, Imprimerie Chaix. He left the press in 1881, although he continued to design posters.

Designs

Chéret's style is distinctive, and many of his designs are strikingly similar. Lettering dominates many early posters. From around 1885, his focus shifted from lettering to figures and products, and he produced designs for a wide range of products and events, including beverages, department stores, ice rinks and theatrical productions. These later posters are more exciting and more collectable, and almost invariably feature female subjects. Unlike Mucha (see pp.162-3), who emphasized the sensuality of his female figures, Chéret's are usually depicted as vibrant and lively, and are never nude. Like the advertisement for the Paris newspaper, *Le Figaro*, in the main picture, his later designs are full of movement, with minimal detail. Foreground subjects generally predominate, usually in striking bright colours against a dark or shadowy background.

* Although Chéret produced a few long, thin posters, most of his work is of the same proportions as the *Saxoléine* poster. However, unlike the work of Mucha, the size of Chéret's posters cannot be used as a reliable guide to authenticity.

Value

Chéret's work is quite common, and only a few of his posters are really valuable. Each of his 1,000 poster designs was printed in large numbers, sometimes as many as 10-20,000. Today, most fetch about a quarter to three quarters of the value of the *Figaro* poster, although good examples can command around twice *Figaro's* value. There are no known fakes, and reproductions are usually easy to spot.

Condition

All of Chéret's designs were printed on cheap paper, so condition is very important. Because there are so many on the market, it is worth paying extra for a poster in good condition.

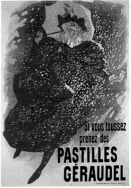

The poster *above*, one of 10 different Chéret posters advertising Geraudel's throat pastilles, is an early design, from c.1890. However, the piece already displays characteristics typical of Chéret's work, such as strong colours and an emphasis on the foreground subject.
* Posters are signed and sometimes dated, but should also bear the name of the printer, Chaix. Other designers used Chaix, but none produced work as accomplished or as valuable.

Chéret often produced more than one poster to advertise a type of merchandise (as happens with today's products). The example *above*, recommending Saxoléine, a popular brand of kerosene (lamp oil), is one of 14 different designs advertising the product.

Bec Auer, *an advertising poster designed by T. Privat-Livemont 1896; 31in x 42in/78.8cm x 108cm; value code C*

Identification checklist for Privat-Livemont's posters
1. Is the poster promoting a commodity, a seaside resort or an exhibition?
2. Is the subject a woman with flowing robes and hair?
3. Does any decoration include organic motifs such as branches, leaves or sunflowers?
4. Is any lettering in the distinctive Art Nouveau style?
5. Is the palette of red, green and blue or, alternatively, earthy neutral tones?

T. Privat-Livemont (Belgian, 1861-1936)
Privat-Livemont opened a design studio in 1890. Like most poster designers of the period, his work was promotional, for products such as tea, biscuits, chocolate, corsets, cocoa and alcohol, especially Absinthe Robette.

The poster *above* is advertising Auer light, a type of gas lamp mantle with an extra-bright light. Privat-Livemont also promoted seaside resorts and exhibitions. His work is often compared to that of Mucha (see pp.162-3), but his designs are rarely as sensual as Mucha's.

Like Mucha's, Privat-Livemont's subjects are usually women, often with flowing hair, and may appear semi-nude or semi-veiled. Some figures are romanticized – in the poster *above*, entitled *Pépiniéristes*, the figures hardly look like the nursery gardeners they are intended to be. His subjects can appear slightly strange: the clumsy, frowning features of the woman in the *Bec Auer* poster run counter to the typical advertising beauty of the time. Figures can also be anatomically incorrect, perhaps with excessively curved backs or drawn out of perspective.

Motifs

Typically Art Nouveau motifs recur, such as sunflowers, and the robes of the *pépiniéristes* echo the work of the pre-Raphaelites. The palette reflects the organic preoccupation of Art Nouveau, with tones of red, green and blue, or earthy neutrals.

Verification and valuation

Privat-Livemont used cheap paper and his work is usually signed and often dated. Posters were always made to precise measurements, which can be checked if there is any doubt. His work is not known to have been faked, and reproductions are obvious. His posters are rare and popular. Those he produced to promote absinthe are especially sought after, particularly in the United States.

EUGÈNE SAMUEL GRASSET (Swiss, 1841-1917)

This Swiss-born architect and designer was influenced by Pre-Raphaelite art, medieval architecture and Japanese art. He settled in Paris where he designed posters featuring feminine, old-fashioned women, unlike the more stylized and modern female subjects of other Art Nouveau posterists. The woman in the lithograph *below* hides demurely behind a fan.

This poster shows Grasset's typical, somewhat limited palette of bold, strong tones of yellow, green and blue, outlined in black.
* Some Grasset posters have been later backed with linen, to strengthen the inferior paper.
* Grasset is not currently popular and good examples of his work can be acquired for very little. Being rare, a certain amount of damage is acceptable and strength of colour will always be a more important consideration than condition.

Marks

Grasset's signature usually consists of a capital ''EG'' followed by ''rasset'' (see *below*). The mark may appear in reverse. Most of his work was printed by Chaix de Malherbes, the printer used by Chéret (see pp.166-7).

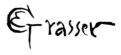

THEOPHILE STEINLEN

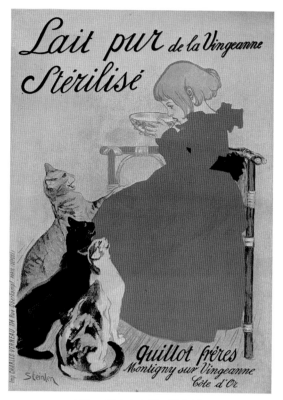

A lithographic poster by Theophile Steinlen
1894; 55 × 38½in/140 × 98cm; value code B

Identification checklist for the posters of Theophile Steinlen

1. Is the palette strong, varied and well balanced?
2. Does the poster depict a scene from typical contemporary Parisian life?
3. Is there a predominance of lettering?
4. Are animals, particularly cats, featured?
5. Is the poster signed?

Theophile-Alexandre Steinlen (Swiss-born, naturalized French, 1859-1923)
Steinlen came to Paris in 1881. As a youth, he adopted socialist ideals, partly influenced by the novels of the French writer, Emile Zola. As an artist, he attempted to portray the daily life of the ordinary people of Paris. His work is not as well-documented as that of some of his more commercially-orientated contemporaries. He is known for doing some commercial work, but was foremost an artist and painter. He was greatly influenced by Toulouse-Lautrec.

Typical features

All of Steinlen's posters were well-executed and feature a well-blended variety of good, strong colours.

A catophile, Steinlen was particularly fond of drawing cats; the poster in the main picture, advertising milk, typically features cats. Dogs are also common. Many subjects can be identified: the girl in the milk poster is Steinlen's daughter, Collette. His work is always signed, either with a monogram or simply "STEINLEN".

Collecting

He designed numerous war posters, and posters with a social message, such as those bearing the legend "Save the Children", but these are primarily collected only by a few specialists and museums and are of little commercial value.

* Like his contemporaries, Steinlen used cheap paper, and little of his work survives in good condition. However, not being prolific, condition is not crucial.
* Steinlen has not been faked, but his work has been reproduced. With age, some well-executed reproductions can look original.

The half-clothed figure in this poster, *above*, caused a tremendous outcry when it appeared. Steinlen produced another version with the figure dressed, which is rarer but not much more expensive than the "undressed" version. The poster advertises the serialization of a contemporary novel about the white slave trade: "La traite des blanches" translates as "white slavery".

The poster *above* advertises a Parisian printing service, Charles Verneau, and was, obviously enough, printed by the self-same firm, which was responsible for many other Steinlen posters. However, Steinlen also used other printers, most notably Ch. Wall & Cie, Paris. This example displays the characteristically strong, varied and well-blended coloration of Steinlen's work.

* Steinlen is collected more by poster collectors than by print collectors.

Secession, a lithograph designed by Josef Maria Olbrich 1898; 29in × 18in/75.5cm × 46.5 cm; value code A/B

Identification checklist for the Secessionist posters
1. Is the image powerful and striking?
2. Is the design angular and geometrically inspired (as opposed to whimsical)?
3. Are the colours bold, if perhaps somewhat faded?
4. Are any graphics or lettering strongly defined?
5. Is the paper quality poor?
6. Is the work signed?

The Secessionists
The Secession was the term given to the rebellion against established artistic taste which surfaced in Munich, Berlin and Vienna toward the end of the 19thC, and was influenced by the Glasgow School (see pp.28-9), especially Charles Rennie Mackintosh. The Vienna Secession was formed in 1897, by disillusioned members of the Viennese Society of Visual Arts; from 1899, the group, including Josef Olbrich, Josef Hoffmann, Otto Wagner and Koloman

Moser, worked from a new building called the Ver Sacrum, shown in the poster in the main picture, where they also exhibited their work. Both building and poster were designed by Olbrich.

The Secessionists' posters display strong, geometric motifs, bold colouring and geometric graphics. The distinctive lettering evident on both the posters shown here is characteristic of the Secessionists. Both examples advertise Secessionist exhibitions, but posters were also designed for other occasions. The sharp geometric lines were strikingly different from the flowing organic style of other poster designers of the period and set a style that was to influence artists well into the Art Deco period.

Secessionist poster designers

The principal Secessionist designers were Moser, Olbrich, Ferdinand Andri, Gustav Klimt and Alfred Roller. Although not actually Secessionist, the severe, angular style of Charles Rennie Mackintosh was also significant but his work is extremely rare today. Examples by his followers at the Glasgow School were very influential, particularly following the Eighth Secessionist Exhibition at Munich in 1900, and are more common today. Their designs tend not to include writing.

Availability and value

As an innovative, intellectual movement, the Vienna Secessionists appealed to an exclusive market within the limits of Vienna itself; hence, relatively few copies of their posters were produced. The influence of the Secessionists on subsequent art movements has made their work highly sought after and it rarely comes up for sale today.

Examples of their work will be costly, whatever their condition, although perfect examples will raise the highest prices. Faded colours will obviously lower a poster's value – the gold in the main poster has faded relatively badly, although the black is still strikingly bold. Paper quality is also important – the Austrians used better quality paper than the French, but it is still not of high quality.

Marks

Olbrich's poster is clearly marked but other artists' marks are not so obvious. The printer's name usually appears in the same lettering, with the words "Druck..." ("printed by") and "Wein" (Vienna). The few printers used by the Secessionists included A. Berger and Gesellschaft Für Graphische Industrie.

The Austrian painter, Koloman Moser (1868-1918), designed the poster *above* in 1903 for the *Ver Sacrum* journal of posters by the Secessionists. The lines are typically angular, and the image striking, with the writing given as much emphasis as the picture. The three figures, representing writing, painting and music, are integral to the design. The execution is characteristically precise.

MAXFIELD PARRISH

The Spirit of Night, *a calender designed by Maxfield Parrish c.1919; 38 × 18 in/45.5 × 96.5cm; value code G*

Identification checklist for the posters designed of Maxfield Parrish
1. Does the image appear symbolistic?
2. Does it convey a dreamy or fantastic quality?
3. Are the colours unnatural and vividly contrasted, possibly including a violet blue?
4. Is the piece signed or monogrammed?
5. Does the print show evidence of mass-production?

Value point
Parrish's original artwork is extremely rare and commands prices comparable to that of the minor Impressionists.

Maxfield Parrish (American, 1870-1966)

Parrish's work is the best example of American Art Nouveau applied to commercial art. At the Pennsylvania Acadamy of Fine Arts he learned modern printing methods, such as the chromo-lithographic process. He designed theatre sets, book illustrations and typography, as well as magazine covers for *Harper's*, *Life*, and *Scribners Magazine*. However, what is mostly available today is his mass-produced graphic art, including posters, labels and calendars; the example in the main picture was designed for the General Electric Company.

Designs

Parrish combined European theories of symbolism with American imagery, and set androgynous, often naked, beauties or fantastic medieval characters against American landscapes. He adapted symbolic figures to the advertising medium; the woman on the calendar, representing the *Spirit of Night*, is illuminated by new-fangled light made by the General Electric Company. Her simple gown, and the garb of her attendants, have a medieval influence. The deep violet of this background was common.

Chromo-lithographic prints

Maxfield Parrish's best known and most collectable work is a series of chromo-lithographic prints published between 1900 and 1925 by a number of companies, including New York Graphics, Charles Scribner & Sons, Reinthal and Newman, and the Edward Gross Company, New York. The borders of a print may bear a company mark, a facsimile of Parrish's signature, and, very occasionally, an edition number.

EDWARD PENFIELD (American, 1866-1925)

Edward Penfield has been called America's premier poster artist. Like Parrish, he is best known as a commercial graphic artist and book illustrator but, unlike Parrish, he used traditional printing methods such as woodblock and lino cuts. Between 1891 and 1901 Penfield was art director for the prestigious *Harper's Magazine*.

Each year between 1893 and 1901, Penfield produced advertising posters for *Harper's*. Some show the influence of European poster artists; the influence of Toulouse-Lautrec (see pp.164-5) can be seen in the example *above*, in style, subject matter and palette. Penfield's monogram seen here in the top left hand corner, is clearly inspired by Lautrec.

LEYENDECKER, FRANK X. AND JOSEPH C. (American, 1877-1924 and 1874-1951)

The Leyendecker brothers were prolific commercial and graphic

artists. Their styles combine the realism of illustrative art with Art Nouveau elements, such as the subject of the poster *above*, called *Butterfly Girl*, by Frank, the elder brother. Their palettes and motifs echo Maxfield Parrish's work, and American imagery predominates. Original artwork is common. It is really only signed pen and ink drawings, oil and gouache paintings that are of value.

GLOSSARY

Acid cutting A method of decorating glass by which an object is coated with wax or another acid-resistant substance, then incised with a fine steel point and dipped in acid.

"Alexandrite" A glass type named after a greenish gemstone that seems to change to red or reddish-brown in certain light. Lalique (see pp.130-1) sold glasswares of the same name, which possessed these attributes.

Arts and Crafts A late-19thC artistic movement, led by William Morris, which advocated a return to medieval standards of craftsmanship and simplicity of design.

Batik A form of stylized animal and floral design inspired by Javanese textiles.

Bentwood Solid or laminated wood steamed and bent into a curvilinear shape. First used in the 18thC, it was favoured by Wiener Werkstätte craftsmen.

Biscuit The term for unglazed porcelain fired only once.

Britannia metal A 19thC pewter substitute, an alloy of tin, antimony and a trace of copper.

Burmese ware The name under which Thomas Webb & Sons sold their version of Peachblow, a type of American art glass made by combining gold and uranium oxides, patented in 1885 by Mount Washington Glass Works.

Cameo glass Decorative glass formed by laminating together two or more layers of glass, often of varying colours, which are wheel-carved or etched to make a design in relief.

Cased glass (overlay) Similar to cameo glass, but with the design on the outer layer cut away rather than in relief.

Chasing A method of embossing or engraving metal, especially silver.

Cire perdue (''lost wax'') The French term for a process of casting sculpture that results in unique casts.

Cold painting A technique for decorating bronze whereby coloured enamels are annealed or painted on.

Earthenware The term for pottery not vitrified (i.e. treated to achieve a glassy surface). Hence, all pottery except stoneware.

Ebonized wood Wood stained to resemble ebony.

Entrelac A type of interlaced decoration used on jewelry. Of Celtic origin, its use was revived by Arts and Crafts designers.

Etching A type of engraving in which the design, drawn with a needle on a copper plate coated with an acid-resistant, is dipped in acid, then used to transfer ink to paper.

Favrile From the Old English word meaning ''hand-made'', the term for a type of iridescent glass developed by Tiffany.

Glaze The smooth, shiny coating to soft-paste porcelain or stoneware.

Hallmark The marks stamped on silver or gold pieces when passed at assay (the test for quality).

Hard-paste porcelain Porcelain made using the ancient Chinese combination of kaolin and petuntse.

Impressed Indented, as opposed to incised.

Incised Decoration or maker's mark cut or scratched into the surface, rather than impressed.

Intaglio carving A type of carving whereby decoration is carved into a surface; as opposed to relief carving.

Jugendstil The term for German and Austrian design in the Art Nouveau style. Named after the Munich-based publication, *Jugend*.

Letterpress A printing method whereby ink is transferred from raised surfaces to paper by pressure.

Limed oak Oak coated with lime which is then brushed off to leave a white residue in the grain.

Lithograph A print taken from a stone on which a design is drawn in ink and fixed. The remaining porous areas are treated with water so that the printing ink adheres only to the design, which is then transferred to paper.

Lustreware Pottery with a metallic surface produced using metallic oxides, usually silver or copper.

Maquette A rough wax or clay model for a sculpture.

Marqueterie de verre A glassmaking process whereby pieces of coloured glass are pressed into the warm, soft body of a piece and rolled in.

Marquetry Furniture decoration

in which shapes are cut into a sheet of wood veneer and inlaid with other woods or materials.

Martelé French for "hammered"; the term for silverware with a fine hammered surface produced first in France and revived by the American Gorham Corporation during the Art Nouveau period.

Millefiori A glassmaking technique whereby canes of coloured glass are arranged in bundles so that the cross-section creates a pattern. Slices of *millefiori* canes can be used as decoration, or fused together to form hollow wares.

Parian Porcelain with a semi-matt, white body resembling marble, developed as a substitute for the white biscuit figures popularized by Sèvres and others in the 18th and early 19thC.

Pâte-de-cristal Near-transparent glass made of powdered glass paste which has been fused in a mould.

Pâte-de-verre Translucent glass similar to *pâte-de-cristal* but with a lower proportion of lead.

Pâte-sur-pâte A form of ceramic decoration developed at Sèvres (see pp.78-9) whereby white slip is applied and fired in layers, building up a cameo effect.

Patination Alteration to the surface appearance of metal caused by time, use or chemical corrosion.

Planished A smooth finish to metalwork achieved by hammering or rolling.

Plique-à-jour An enamelling method whereby a backed, many-celled mould is filled with translucent enamel of different colours. When the backing is removed, the finished piece resembles stained glass.

Pontil mark The mark left by the iron rod upon which some glass is supported for final shaping after blowing.

Repoussé The term describing relief metalwork decoration created by hammering on the reverse side.

Reticulated Thinly-walled porcelain pieces with intricate pierced decoration produced by Worcester Royal Porcelain in the late 19thC.

Sand-cast A method of casting bronze in a mould made from pounded quartz and sand.

Secessionist The term for the movement formed in opposition to established artistic taste which surfaced in Munich, Berlin and Vienna toward the end of the 19thC, and which sparked the Art Nouveau movement.

Sgraffito A form of earthenware decoration incised through slip, revealing the ground beneath.

Shagreen A type of untanned leather, originally made from the skin of the shagri, a Turkish wild ass, soaked in lime water and dyed. By the 19thC it was made mainly of shark skin.

Signed in the stone or **in the block** A term describing a poster or print the signature of which is designed as a part of the stone from which it was printed.

Slip A smooth dilution of clay and water used in the making and decoration of pottery.

Slip-trailed decoration A form of ceramic decoration involving thin lines of slip trailed across the body of a piece.

Slipware Earthenware decorated with designs trailed in or incised through slip.

Socle The block or slab that forms the lowest part of the pedestal of a sculpture or decorative vase.

Soft-paste porcelain Porcelain made using a combination of kaolin and powdered glass, soapstone or calcined bone.

Stilt mark The mark left on the base of some pottery by supports used during firing.

Stoneware Non-porous pottery, a hybrid of earthenware and porcelain, made of clay and a fusible substance.

Studio glass One-off pieces made by designers and glass-makers in collaboration.

Triple *souffle* ("blowout") glass A variation of mould blowing, this method involves the overlaying of glass in the mould and then pumping in air at very high pressure, pressing the glass into the recesses of the mould.

Tubelining A form of ceramic decoration whereby thin trails of slip are applied as outlines to areas of coloured glaze.

Vaseline glass A cloudy, yellow and oily-looking glass, similar in appearance to vaseline, developed during the 19thC.

Vellum Fine calf or lambskin parchment used to cover some furniture or books.

Vase parlante A form of vase the decoration of which includes an engraved quote from a literary work .

SELECTED DESIGNERS, MANUFACTURERS & RETAILERS

Page references in brackets refer to fuller entries and details of marks given elsewhere.

Amstelhoek (1894-1910)
Dutch ceramics, metalwork and furniture workshop.

Artificers' Guild (1901-1942)
London-based metalworking firm founded by **Nelson Dawson.**

E. Bakalowits & Söhne (est'd 1845)
Viennese glass retailer of avant-garde pieces by designers such as **Koloman Moser.** (pp.58-9)

Barnsley, Sydney (1865-1926), and Ernest (1863-1926)
Furniture designers and co-founders of the **Bath Cabinet Makers Co. Ltd.** Pieces unmarked. (pp.34-5)

Bayes, Gilbert (1872-1953)
English sculptor in a style that combined Art Nouveau and medieval influences. (p.125)

Bergman, Franz (dates unknown)
Austrian sculptor of cold-painted bronzes.

Bing & Grondahl Porcellaensfabrik (1853-present)
Danish producer of porcelain and stoneware in the 18thC and Art Nouveau styles. (p.95)

Bing, Siegfried (1838-1905)
Parisian publisher, art dealer and sponsor. (pp. 16-7)

Boucheron, Maison (1858-present)
Parisian jewelry firm; produced designs mainly for the French and American markets.

Bouval, Maurice (d.1920)
French sculptor and metalworker; made bronze lamps and busts of female figures. (pp.114-5)

Bugatti, Carlo (1855-1940)
Italian furniture designer and craftsman. (pp.24-5)

Bugatti, Rembrandt (1885-1916)
Italian animalier known for bronze wildlife sculptures. (pp.122-3)

Burgun, Schverer (1711-present)
The only German producer of Art Nouveau cameo glass. (pp.44-5)

Carder, Frederick (1864-1963)
British-born glass designer for **Stevens & Williams** and later Art Director at **Steuben.** (pp.72-3)

Chalon, Louis (dates unknown)
French sculptor, whose wares usually feature a female figure. (pp.114-5)

Chéret, Jules (1836-1932)
French commercial graphic artist credited with fathering the modern poster. (pp.166-7)

Christian, Desiré (b. 1846)
French glass designer. Chief artistic designer at **Burgun, Schverer;** opened firm with his brother and son. (p.45)

Colenbrander, Theodorus A.C. (1841-1930)
Dutch porcelain decorator and designer for **Rozenburg.**

Colonna, Edward (b. 1862)
German architect and designer associated with the Paris School.

Cotswold School
Association of English furniture designers, led by Ernest Gimson and the Barnsleys. (pp.30-1)

Couper, James & Sons (dates unknown)
Scottish glassmaking firm known for "Clutha" glass. (pp.62-3)

Dammouse, Albert (1848-1926)
Glassmaker and master of *pâte-de-verre.* Mark: impressed. (p.55)

Daum Frères (1875-present)
Nancy glassworks founded by brothers, Auguste and Antonin made; fine vases and lamps. Marks: relief cut, etched or painted. (pp.50-1)

Dawson, Nelson (1859-1942)
English painter, silversmith, jeweler and co-founder of the **Artificers' Guild.**

de Feure, Georges (1868-1928)
French furniture, metalwork, fabric and ceramics designer associated with the Paris School style of Art Noveau (pp.16-7).

Mark: signature, either painted or etched.

Denislow, William Walter (dates unknown)
American metalwork designer associated with the **Roycrofters.**

Doat, Taxile (b. 1851)
French porcelain designer and decorator for Sèvres. (p.79)

Doulton & Co (1815-present)
London-based producer of stoneware and porcelain figures. Marks: printed, impressed or painted. (pp.102-3)

Durand, Victor (1870-1931)
American glass artist. Produced primarily iridescent wares for the **Vineland Glass Co.**

Ellis, Harvey (1852-1904)
English-born architect and designer associated with **Gustav Stickley.**

Farhner, Theodor (1868-1928)
German jeweler; mass-produced fine jewelry in an abstract Art Nouveau style. (p.143)

Feuillâtre, Eugène (1870-1916)
French designer of jewelry; specialized in *plique-à-jour* enamel. Mark: engraved. (p.135)

Fisher, Alexander (1864-1936)
English enamelling artist known for fine silver plaques. (p.155)

Foley (later Shelley) (1892-1925)
Staffordshire pottery; producer of decorative earthenwares and bone china. (p.101)

Fouquet, Georges (1862-1957)
Innovative French jewelery designer. (pp.132-3)

Gaillard, Eugène (active 1895-1911)
French furniture designer and associate of the **Paris School.**

Gaillard, Lucien (b. 1861)
French jeweler and silversmith, famous for fine hand-made work in unusual materials. (pp.134-5)

Gallé, Emile (1846-1904)
French designer and glass-worker; considered the greatest of glass craftsmen. (p.46-9).

Gilbert, Sir Alfred (1854-1934)
English sculptor who marks the first transition from the Victorian style to Art Nouveau (p.124-5).

Goldscheider, Marcel (1855-1953)
Viennese ceramics manufacturer; mass-produced Art Nouveau vases.

Gorham Corporation (1813-present)
Largest 19thC American silver producer. (pp.156-7)

Grasset, Eugène Samuel (1841-1917)
Swiss-born architect, designer and posterist. (p.169)

Greene Brothers
American furniture designers. Worked to commission, mainly in Honduras mahogany. (pp.36-7)

Grueby Faience Company (1894-1930)
Boston-based producer of tin-glazed earthenware and faience. (pp.106-7)

Guild of Handicraft (1888-1908)
British silverworking guild famous for silverware. (pp.154-5)

Gurschner, Gustav (b. 1873)
Bavarian sculptor and metalworker. (pp.126-7)

Handel (1885-1936)
American glassworks. (pp.74-5)

Harris, Kate (active c.1890-1910)
English metalwork designer in the Art Nouveau style. (p.153)

Henry, J.S. (c.1880-c.1900)
London cabinet-maker. (p.34)

Hoffmann, Josef (1870-1956)
Architect, designer, and founder member of the Vienna Secession.

Hueck, Eduard (est'd 1864)
German metalwork firm. Some wares designed by **Olbrich.**

Hutton, William & Sons (1800-1923)
English producer of silver, pewter and Britannia metal. (pp.152-3)

Jensen, Georg (1866-1935)
Danish silversmith and sculptor. (pp.144-5)

Kayser Sohn (1894-c.1904)
German metalwork foundry. (p.141)

King, Jessie Marion (1876-1949)
Scottish illustrator and designer of ceramics and jewelry,

179

including designs for Liberty's Cymric range.

JESSIE·M·KING

Kipp, Karl (dates unknown)
American metalworker and designer in the Secessionist style. Director of the **Roycrofters** from 1908.

Knox, Archibald (1864-1933)
Manx metalwork designer, notably of Liberty's Cymric range. (pp.146-51).

Korschann, Charles (b. 1872)
Bohemian sculptor, mainly of female figural bronzes. (pp.120-1)

Lalique, René (1860-1945)
French master jeweler of the Art Nouveau period. Marks: "R Lalique" (*below*) used during his lifetime, the "R" being dropped after his death.

R LALIQUE

Laporte-Blairsy, Leo (1865-1923)
French sculptor of functional yet decorative pieces, especially lighting. (pp.118-9)

Larche, Raoul-François (1860-1912)
French sculptor known for gilt-bronze female figures. (pp.116-7)

Läuger, Max (1864-1952)
German architect, engineer, sculptor and ceramist. (pp.80-1)

Legras (1864-present)
French glassmaking firm; produced cameo wares and commercial glass similar to **Daum** and **Müller Frères**.

Léonard, Agathon (b. 1841)
French ceramicist and sculptor. Made Art Nouveau-style biscuit figures and gilt-bronze statuettes. (p.117)

A Leonard ScLp

Leyendecker, Frank and Joseph (1877-1924; 1874-1951)
Prolific American commercial and graphic artists in a distinctively American style. (p.175)

Liberty (1875-present)
English retail firm established by Arthur Lasenby Liberty to sell fine British-made goods and Oriental art and fabrics, later

expanding to include ceramics, metalwork and furniture. (pp.146-9)

Liisberg C.F. (1860-1909)
Danish ceramicist and decorator at **Royal Copenhagen.**

Loetz (1836-1939)
Bohemian producers of high-quality art glass. (pp.56-7)

Macintyre & Co. (1847-present)
Staffordshire pottery; employed **William Moorcroft** as a designer.

Mackintosh, Charles Rennie (1868-1928)
Scottish architect and designer. Formed the "Glasgow Four" with **Margaret Mackintosh**, Frances Macdonald and J.H.McNair. (pp.28-9)

Mackintosh, Margaret M. (1865-1933)
Designer and metalworker, wife of **C.R. Mackintosh** and member of the "Glasgow Four".

MMM

Marcus, Herman (dates unknown)
Finest American jeweler of the Art Nouveau period; founded Marcus and Co. in 1900 and perfected the *plique-à-jour* method of enamelling.

Masriera Brothers (1872-1958)
Spanish jewelers influenced by French Art Nouveau, particularly the work of **Lalique.**

Massier, Clement (1845-1917)
French ceramicist and producer of earthenware with iridescent or lustre decoration.

Meissen (c.1710-present)
Prominent German ceramic factory; traditional forms were applied with Art Nouveau decoration. (pp.84-5)

Meyr's Neffe (est'd 1815)
Bohemian glassworks; produced useful wares of geometric inspiration.

Mintons, Ltd (1793-present)
Staffordshire pottery; produced earthenware, art pottery and porcelain. Marks: printed. (pp.100-1)

Moorcroft, William (1872-1945)
Head of Art Pottery Department of the Staffordshire pottery, **Macintyre & Co.** Best known for "Florian" ware vases. Mark: signature or monogram. (pp.98-9)

Moser, Koloman (1868-1918)
Austrian artist and designer of furniture, ceramics and glass; founder member of the Vienna Secession and co-founder of the **Wiener Werkstätte** (p.139).

Mucha, Alphonse (1860-1939)
Czech artist commissioned by the actress Sarah Bernhardt to design posters, stage sets and costumes. (pp.162-3)

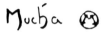

Muller, Albin (1871-1941)
German architect and designer known for useful stonewares with moulded decoration. (p.81)
Müller Frères (active c.1900-36)
French glassmaking firm run by Henri and Désiré Müller. Marks: etched or relief cut. (pp.52-3)

Murrle Bennet & Co. (1884-1914)
Anglo-German mass-producer of jewelry. Marks: stamped.

Nancy School
A group of artists and designers inspired by the work of **Gallé and Majorelle** in Nancy towards the end of the 19thC. (pp.14-5)
Newcomb College Pottery (c.1895-1945)
American producer of art pottery, such as vases and tea wares with incised floral patterns.
Ohr, George E. (1857-1918)
American studio art potter and founder of the Biloxi Art Pottery in Mississippi. Impressed marks. (pp.108-9)

G. E. OHR, BILOXI.

Olbrich, Josef Maria (1867-1908)
Architect, designer and founder of the Vienna Secession. (p.138-9)

Owens, J.B. (d. 1934)
American potter and founder of J. B. Owens Pottery at Roseville, Ohio. (pp.104-5)

Palme-König (est'd 1786)
Bohemian glassmakers; produced fine-quality Art Nouveau iridescent glass wares and table glass in forms popularized by **Loetz.**
Paris School
The term for those artists and designers associated with the Parisian publisher and dealer, **Siegfried Bing.** (pp.16-7)
Parrish, Maxfield (1870-1966)
American posterist, illustrator and theatrical designer in the Art Nouveau style. (pp.174-5)
Pèche, Dagobert (1887-1923)
Austrian artist and designer of ceramics and metalwork, and co-director of the **Wiener Werkstätte.**

Penfield, Edward (1866-1925)
American graphic artist, posterist and illustrator. (p.175)
Powell, Harry J. (active c.1880-c.1910)
English glass artist and designer; director of Powell & Sons between 1880 and 1914. (pp.62-3)
Powell, James & Sons (c.1830-1980)
Innovative London glasshouse, influential during the late 19thC. Acquired **Whitefriars Glassworks** in 1833. (pp.62-3)
Powolny, Michael (1871-1954)
Austrian ceramics decorator and founder of Wiener Keramik factory. Marks: painted or impressed. (pp.82-83)

Privat-Livemont, T. (1861-1936)
Belgian commercial artist and posterist. (pp.168-9)

Prouvé, Victor (1858-1943)
French painter, sculptor and designer in the Art Nouveau style.

Prutscher, Otto (1880-1949)
Designer for **Wiener Werkstätte** of distinctive glass, jewelry and silver. Wares unsigned. (pp.60-1)

Quezal (1901-25)
American glassmaking firm inspired by nearby **Tiffany.** (pp.70-1)

Reissner, Stellmacher and Kessel (R.S.K.) (est'd 1892)
Bohemian ceramics firm; main contribution to Art Nouveau was the "Amphora" range. (pp.86-7)

Ricketts, Charles de Sousy (1866-1931)
English sculptor whose Art Nouveau style was inspired by the work of the Frenchman, Rodin. (pp.124-5)

Rode, Godfred (1862-1937)
Danish ceramic decorator at **Royal Copenhagen.** Famous for underglaze seascapes.

Rohlfs, Charles (1853-1936)
American actor, stove maker and designer of furniture, particularly in oak (pp.36-7). Mark: burned initials.

Rookwood (1880-1960)
Foremost American producer of fine Art Nouveau pottery. (pp.104-5)

Rörstrand (est'd 1726)
Prominent Swedish pottery: producer of bold designs under the influence of French Art Nouveau. (pp.96-7)

Rosenthal, Philip (d. 1937)
German potter and founder of the Rosenthal factory, producer of high-quality tablewares. Marks: printed.

Roseville Company (1890-mid-1940s)
American pottery established on the site of **J.B.Owens'** pottery;

produced wares similar to Rookwood's Standard glazed wares. (pp.104-5)

Royal Copenhagen (1775-present)
Danish ceramics factory. Arnold Krog introduced innovative glazing and decorative techniques. (p.94-5)

Royal Dux (1860-mid-20thC)
Bohemian ceramic producer known for classically-inspired figures.

Roycrofters, The (1895-1938)
American craft community founded by Elbert Hubbard (1856-1917) to produce simple furniture in the Mission style, textiles and metalwork. (p.159)

Rozenburg (1883-1916)
Pottery whose "eggshell" porcelain is considered foremost Dutch contribution to Art Nouveau. (pp.88-9)

Sèvres (1750-present)
Renowned French ceramics factory, whose Art Nouveau pieces are acknowledged as the finest of the period. (pp.78-9)

Solon, Leon V. (1872-1957)
English ceramic designer and director of Mintons, 1900-09. (pp.100-1)

Spencer, Edward Napier Hitchcock (1872-1938)
English metalwork designer and co-founder of the **Artificers' Guild.**

Steinlen, Theophile-Alexandre (1859-1923)
Swiss-born, naturalized French, artist and posterist whose work reflected his socialist principles and love of animals, particularly dogs and cats. (pp.170-1)

Steuben (1903-present)
New York-based glassworks founded by Howkes family and **Frederick Carder.** (pp.72-3)

Stevens & Williams (c.1830-present)
Glassmakers at Stourbridge in the English Midlands, best known for fine cameo wares. (pp.64-5)

Stickley brothers (1891-1910)
George and Albert, brothers of **Gustav,** made oak furniture in a style popularized by Gustav, but of inferior quality (pp.38-9).

Stickley, Gustav (1847-1942)
American furniture designer;

produced pieces with an Arts and Crafts feel, notably his range of ''Craftsman furniture''. (pp.38-9).

Stickley L. and J. G. (c.1900-present)
American furniture makers of inferior versions of the designs of their brother, **Gustav Stickley.** (pp.38-9).

Taylor, Ernest A. (1874-1951)
Scottish painter and furniture designer. (pp.32-3)

Teco (c.1902-c.1923)
Part of Gates Potteries, an Illinois terracotta, tile and brick firm founded by William Day Gates. (pp.110-1)

Tiffany, Louis Comfort (1848-1933)
Founder of Louis C. Tiffany in the United States, which initially designed interiors but is now better known for glasswares, particularly lamps. (pp.66-9)

Toft, Albert (1862-1949)
English sculptor of bronze figural pieces, mainly of ethereal, cloaked female subjects. (pp.124-5)

Toulouse-Lautrec, Henri de (1864-1901)
Renowned French commercial artist and posterist; depicted the seedier theatres and nightclubs of Paris. (pp.164-5).

Unger Brothers (1872-c.1910)
American silversmiths and jewelers. Most wares designed by Emma Dickinson (pp.156-7).

Van Briggle, Artus (1869-1904)
American potter and pottery decorator. Worked initially for **Rookwood**; founded the Van Briggle Pottery Co. in 1902.

Van de Hoef, Christian Johannes 1875-1933)
Dutch sculptor, medallist and ceramicist, the main designer at **Amstelhoek.** Mark: painted.

Van de Velde, Henri (1863-1957)
Belgian architect and designer; worked with **Siegfried Bing** and at **Meissen.** (pp.18-9)

Van Erp, Dirk (1860-1953)
Dutch-born metalworker; (pp.158-9).

Vever (1821-1982)
Leading French Art Nouveau retail and manufacturing jewelers. (pp.136-7)

Villeroy and Boch (1836-present)
German producer of stoneware art pottery.

Vineland Glass Manufacturing Company (dates unknown)
American glassmaking firm with strong ties with **Quezal.**

Wahliss, Ernst (1863-1930)
Bohemian potter influenced by **Michael Powolny.**

Walter, Alméric (1859-1942)
French Art Nouveau glass artist; worked primarily in *pâte-de-verre.*

Webb, Thomas & Son (1856-present)
Stourbridge-based glassworks whose Art Nouveau glass includes Burmese ware, cameo glass and overlay wares. (pp.64-5)

Weduwe N.S.A. Brantjes & Co. (1895-1904)
Dutch ceramics factory. (pp.90-1)

Whitefriars Glass Works (c.1680-present)
Influential London glasshouse bought by **James Powell & Sons** in 1833. (pp.62-3)

Wiener Werkstätte (Vienna Workshops) (1903-32)
Series of Austrian craft workshops founded by **Kolomon Moser** and **Josef Hoffmann,** (pp.22-3, 60-1, 138-9, 172-3).

Wüttembergischer Metallwarenfabrik (W.M.F.) (1880-present)
Austrian metalwork foundry; made decorative and domestic metalwork. Marks: stamped.

Zijl, Lambertus (dates unknown)
Dutch sculptor and ceramicist employed by **Amstelhoek.**

Zsolnay (est'd 1862)
Hungarian ceramics firm; helped the development of Art Nouveau in eastern Europe. (pp.92-3)

BIBLIOGRAPHY

GENERAL

Adburgham, Alison, et al, *Liberty's 1875-1975*, catalogue of an exhibition at the Victoria and Albert Museum, London, 1975

Liberty's: A Biography of a Shop, London, 1975

Amaya, Mario, *Art Nouveau*, London and New York, 1966

Anscombe, Isabelle and Charlotte Gere, *Arts and Crafts in Britain and America*, London, 1978

Aslin, Elizabeth, *The Aesthetic Movement, Prelude to Art Nouveau*, London, 1969

Battersby, Martin, *The World of Art Nouveau*, London, 1968

Becker, Vivienne, *Art Nouveau Jewelry*, London, 1985

Bröhan, Karl H., *Kunsthandwerk I. Jugendstil, Werkbund – Art Deco*, Berlin 1976

Clarke, Robert Judson, *The Arts and Crafts Movement in America 1876-1916*, Exhibition Catalogue, Princeton, 1972

Aspects of the Arts and Crafts Movement in America, Record of the Art Museum, Princeton University, Vol. 34, No. 2, 1975

Cooper Hewitt Museum, *Vienna Moderne 1898-1918*, New York, 1978

Duncan, Alistair, *Louis Majorelle – Master of Art Nouveau Design*, London, 1991

Exhibition Catalogue, *Art and Design in Europe and America 1800-1900*, Victoria and Albert Museum, London, 1987

Exhibition Catalogue, *Art Nouveau Belgium/France*, Institute for the Arts, Rice University, Houston, 1976

Exhibition Catalogue, *Christopher Dresser 1834-1904*, London, 1972

Exhibition Catalogue, *The Amsterdam School*, Gemeente Museum, the Hague, 1975

Exhibition Catalogue, *Vienna – Turn of the Century*, Fischer Fine Art, London, 1979

Fanelli, Giovanni, and Ezio Godoli, *Art Nouveau Postcards*, New York, 1987

Garner, Philippe, *Phaidon Encyclopedia of Decorative Arts*, Oxford, 1978

Gilbert, Alfred, *Royal Academy of Arts 1986*, Exhibition Catalogue

Halen, Widar, *Christopher Dresser*, Oxford, 1990

Haslam, Malcolm, *Arts and Crafts*, London, 1988

Heller, Carl Benno, *Art Nouveau Furniture*, Kirchdorf, 1990

International Exhibition Foundation, *Art Nouveau Jewelry by René Lalique*, Washington D.C., 1985-1986

Klein, Dan and Margaret Bishop, *Decorative Art 1880-1980*, Oxford, 1986

Leidelmeijer, Frans and Daan van der Cingel, *Art Nouveau and Art Deco in the Netherlands*, Amsterdam, 1983

Marks and Monograms of the Modern Movement 1815-1930, London, 1977

Metropolitan Museum of Art, *In Pursuit of Beauty*, New York, 1986

Morris, Barbara, *Liberty Design*, London, 1989

Neurwirth, Walter, *Wiener Werkstätte*, Vienna 1984

Royal Academy, *Vienna Seccession, Art Nouveau to 1970*, London, 1971

Strong, Roy, *The Collector's Encyclopedia Victoriana to Art Deco*, London, 1974

Tilbrook, A.J., *The Designs of Archibald Knox for Liberty & Co.*, London, 1976

Ward Lock, *Dictionary of Turn of the Century Antiques*, London, 1974

Warren, Geoffrey, *All Colour Book of Art Nouveau*, London 1972

Weisberg, Gabriel P., *Art Nouveau Bing – Paris Style 1900*, New York, 1986

CERAMICS

Atterbury, Paul, *Moorcroft Pottery*, London 1987

Dictionary of Minton, Woodbridge, 1989

Austwick, J. and B., *The Decorated Tile*, London, 1980

Batkin, Maureen, *Wedgwood Ceramics, 1846-1959*, London, 1982

Dennis, Richard, *Doulton Stoneware and Terracotta 1870-1925*, London, 1971

Doulton Pottery Stoneware Terracotta 1870-1928, London, 1971

Doulton Pottery Lambeth to Burslem 1873-1939, London, 1975

Royal Doulton 1815-1965, London, 1965

Eyles, Desmond, *The Doulton Lambeth Wares*, 1975

The Doulton Burslem Wares, 1980

Evans, Paul F., *Art Pottery of the United States*, New York, 1974

Exhibition Catalogue, *William Moorcroft and Walter Moorcroft*, London, 1973

Frelinghuysen, Alice Cooney, *American Porcelain 1770-1920*, Metropolitan Museum of Art, New York Exhibition, 1989

Godden, G.A., *An Illustrated Encyclopaedia of British Pottery and Porcelain*, London, 1968

Haslam, Malcolm, *English Art Pottery 1865-1915*, Woodbridge, 1975

Henzke, Lucile, *American Art Pottery*, New Jersey, 1970

Kunst & Antiquilaten, *Rozenburg 1883-1917*, Munich, 1984

Neuwirth, Waltraud, *Osterreichisches Keramik des Jugendstils*, Munich, 1974
Wiener Keramik, Braunschwig, 1974

Peck, Herbert, *The Book of Rookwood Pottery*, New York, 1968

Royal Copenhagen Porcelain, 200 years of., Catalogue of an exhibition circulated by the Smithsonian Institute, 1974-1976

Winstone, Victor, *Royal Copenhagen*, London, 1984

GLASS

Amaya, Mario, *Tiffany Glass*, London, 1967

Davis, Derek C. and Keith Middlemas, *Coloured Glass*, London, 1968

Dodsworth, Roger, *Glass and Glassmakers*, Risborough, 1982

Duncan, Alistair, Martin Eidelburg and Neil Harris, *The Masterworks of Louis Comfort Tiffany*, New York, 1990

Garner, Philippe, *Emile Gallé*, London, 1976

Gardner, Paul V., *The Glass of Frederick Carder*, New York, 1971

Grover, Ray and Lee, *Art Glass Nouveau*, Rutland, Vermont, 1968
Carved and Decorated European Art Glass, Vermont, 1970

Koch, Robert, *Louis C. Tiffany's Glass – Bronzes – Lamps*, New York, 1971
Louis C. Tiffany, Rebel in Glass, New York, 1974

Newark, Tim, *The Art of Emile Gallé*, London, 1989

Paul, Tessa, *The Art of Louis Comfort Tiffany*, London, 1987

Potter, Norman and Douglas Jackson, *Tiffany*, London, 1988

Revi, Albert Christian, *Nineteenth Century Glass, its Genesis and Development*, New York, 1967
American Art Nouveau Glass, Nashville, Tennessee 1968

Wakefield, Hugh, *19th Century British Glass*, London, 1961

FURNITURE

Alison, Filippo, *Charles Rennie Mackintosh – Chairs*, London, 1978

Aslin, Elizabeth, *19th Century English Furniture*, London, 1962

Billcliffe, Roger, *Charles Rennie Mackintosh, Furniture and Interiors*, Guildford 1979

Cooper, Jeremy, *Victorian and Edwardian Furniture and Interiors*, London, 1987

Exhibition Catalogue, *Architect-Designers Pugin to Mackintosh*, The Fine Art Society, London 1981

Hanks, David A., *The Decorative Designs of Frank Lloyd Wright*, London, 1979

JEWELRY

Bayer, Patricia, and Mark Waller, *The Art of René Lalique*, London, 1988

Becker, Vivienne, *The Jewellery of René Lalique*, Exhibition Catalogue, London, 1987

Bury, Shirley, *Jewellery 1789-1910 (Volume II 1862-1910)*, Woodbridge, 1990

Mortimer, Tony, *Lalique Jewellery and Glassware*, London, 1989

LIGHTING

Neustadt, Egon, *The Lamps of Tiffany*, New York, 1970

SCULPTURE

Beattie, Susan, *The New Sculpture*, London, 1983

Cooper, Jeremy, *Nineteenth Century Romantic Bronzes*, Devon, 1974

Handley-Read, Charles, *British Sculpture, 1850-1914*, London, 1968

SILVER AND METALWORK

Blair, Claude, *The History of Silver*, New York, 1987

INDEX

PICTURE CREDITS AND ACKNOWLEDGMENTS

The publishers would like to thank the following auction houses, museums, dealers, collectors and other sources for supplying pictures for use in this book or for allowing their pieces to be photographed.

1 SNY; 3 SL; 10 SNY; 12 CG; 13l SM, 13r CNY; 14 CNY; 15l CNY, 15r SM; 16 SL; 17l SM, 17tr CNY, 17br CM; 18 SM; 19 CNY(x3); 20 CG; 21l SM, 21r SM; 22 CNY; 23l SL, 23rt P, 23rb CNY; 24 SL; 25 CL; 26 CL; 27 SL(x2); 28 SM; 29 SL(x2); 30 FAS; 31t P, 31b P; 32 SL; 33l SL, 33r CL; 34 SL; 35 SL(x2); 36 CNY; 37 CNY(x2); 38 CNY; 39 CNY(x2); 40 CNY; 41 CNY; 42 SM; 44 HF; 45l CG, 45r CNY; 46 CL; 47l CNY, 47r CG; 48l CL, 48tr HF, 48br CM; 49tl SL, 49bl CNY, 49r CL; 50 HF; 51l SM, 51r CNY; 52 SM; 53l CNY, 53r SM; 54 HF; 55 SM; 56 CG; 57l SL, 57r CL; 58 MB; 59l SL, 59tr MB, 59br MB; 60 CAmst; 61l CL, 61t&br CAmst; 62 P; 63 CL(x2); 64 MP; 65 MP(x2); 66 CNY; 67 CNY(x3); 68 SNY(x3); 69tl CNY, 69bl SNY, 69r CNY; 70 CNY; 71l CNY, 71r SNY; 72 SNY; 73l SNY(x2), 73r CNY; 74 Hib; 75 Hib(x3); 76 CG; 78 Sev; 79l Sev, 79r HF; 80 BG; 81l HF, 81r SL; 82 CL; 83l CL, 83r SL; 84 P; 85t SM, 85b MB; 86 SL; 87 SNY; 88 SL; 89l CAmst, 89r SL; 90 V&A; 91 tlCAmst; 91 b&tr NK; 92 CG; 93l CG, 93tr SL, 93br HF; 94 RC; 95l RC, 95r HF; 96 CNY; 97tl CNY, 97bl CNY, 97tr CG; 98 SL; 99 SL(x3); 100 MB; 101 B(x2); 102 CL; 103t P, 103r RD; 104 SNY; 105l Met, 105r CNY; 106 CNY; 107tl DR, 107bl CNY, 107r DR; 108 CNY; 109l CNY, 109r DR; 110 CNY; 111l CNY; 111r CNY; 112 SL; 114 SL; 115 SL(x2); 116 CNY; 117l SL, 117tr SL, 117br SL; 118 SL; 119l SNY, 119r CNY; 120 CL; 121l SL; 121r CL; 122 SG; 123 SG(x2); 124 P; 125l BAL, 125r SL; 126 SL; 127l CNY; 127r B; 128 ??ek; 130 CG; 131l SL, 131r CG; 132 SM; 133tl SL, 133bl SG, 133r SG; 134 CG; 135t SL, 135l CNY, 135r SNY; 136 SL; 137l SL, 137r CG; 138 SM; 139l SL, 139r CNY; 140 SL; 141t SL, 141r RPB; 142 SL; 143 SL(x3); 144 CNY; 145l CNY, 145r SL; 146 SL; 147 SL(x3); 148 SL(x3); 149 SL(x3); 150 SL; 151l SL, 151r CNY(x2); 152 NH; 153l SL, 153r NH; 154 SL; 155l SL, 155r SL; 156 CNY; 157l CNY; 158 CNY; 159 CNY(x2); 160 JR; 162 CNY; 163 SL(x2); 164 CSK; 165l CNY, 165r CSK; 166 CL; 167 CL(x2); 168 RB; 169 CSK(x2); 170 P; 171t P, 171b CSK; 172 P; 173t P, 173b CSK; 174 P; 175tr CSK, 175br CSK; jacket CNY

KEY
b bottom, c centre, l left, r right, t top

B	Bonham's, London		to the Broadfield
BAL	Bridgeman Art Library		House Glass Museum,
BG	Bethnal Green Museum		Kingswinford,
C	Christie's, London		Stourbridge
CAmst	Christie's, Amsterdam	ND	Nicholas Dawes
CG	Christie's, Geneva	NH	The Nicholas Harris
CNY	Christie's, New York		Gallery, London
CSK	Christie's, South	NK	Nederlands
	Kensington		Keramiekmuseum,
DR	David Rago Arts and		Leeuwarden
	Crafts, New Jersey	P	Phillips, London
FAS	Fine Art Society	RB	Richard Barclay
HF	Habsburg Feldman	RC	Royal Copenhagen
Hib	John and Carole Hibel	RD	Royal Doulton
	– H & D Press, Inc	RPB	The Royal Pavilion,
JR	Jack Rennart		Brighton
MB	Mitchell Beazley	S	Sotheby's, London
Met	Metropolitan Museum	Sev	Le Pavillon de Sèvres
	of Art, New York		Ltd, London
MP	Michael Parkington	SM	Sotheby's, Monaco
	Collection, on loan	SNY	Sotheby's, New York

Thanks also to Barbara Morris for her help in the preparation of this book.